Jessie Fothergill

Borderland

A country-town chronicle. Vol. 3

Jessie Fothergill

Borderland
A country-town chronicle. Vol. 3

ISBN/EAN: 9783337344252

Printed in Europe, USA, Canada, Australia, Japan

Cover: Foto ©Andreas Hilbeck / pixelio.de

More available books at **www.hansebooks.com**

BORDERLAND:

A COUNTRY-TOWN CHRONICLE.

BY

JESSIE FOTHERGILL,

AUTHOR OF "THE FIRST VIOLIN," "KITH AND KIN," "PROBATION,"
"THE WELLFIELDS," AND "HEALEY."

IN THREE VOLUMES.
VOL. III.

LONDON:

RICHARD BENTLEY AND SON,

𝔓𝔲𝔟𝔩𝔦𝔰𝔥𝔢𝔯𝔰 𝔦𝔫 𝔒𝔯𝔡𝔦𝔫𝔞𝔯𝔶 𝔱𝔬 𝔥𝔢𝔯 𝔐𝔞𝔧𝔢𝔰𝔱𝔶 𝔱𝔥𝔢 𝔔𝔲𝔢𝔢𝔫.

1886.

CONTENTS OF VOL. III.

— ⚬ —

BORDERLAND.

CHAPTER I.

A FALSE STEP IN GOOD FAITH.

THE day after that unfortunate fracas at
the mills was Christmas Day. It will
easily be understood that to Roger it did
not this year form the most cheerful occasion imaginable. He had seen Ada on
the evening of the twenty-fourth, and some
kind of a reconciliation had then been
patched up between them, but one which
set Roger thinking, and made him feel that
many differences of opinion might be less
disastrous than such a making up of a
quarrel. It had not been spontaneous; it
had been largely due to the intervention

of Mr. Dixon, who was very indignant with his daughter for what he called "making such an exhibition of herself." He condemned Otho Askam in no measured terms, but his blame of Ada and her "want of sense" was almost as strong. He wanted to know where she meant to draw the line in her folly. He added that she was doing her character no good by such "carryings on," and uttered a dark hint as to the implacable nature of his wrath should she ever in the future disgrace, or as he expressed it, "lower herself" in any way whatsoever.

During the paternal admonitions Mrs. Dixon maintained an ominous silence. As has been before said, she did not favour Roger's pretensions, and had always looked to her daughter to marry well ;—not what Mr. Dixon considered to be well, but what she, his consort, understood by the term. On returning from the concert, and finding that Ada had gone to her room, her mother had repaired thither, and had extracted

from the girl an account of every word
uttered throughout the evening, by herself,
Otho, Miss Wynter, and Roger. She had
not said much, save some strong expres-
sions condemnatory of Roger's behaviour,
which she characterized as " tyrannical,"
" impudent," " masterful," and " odious,"
and expressed indignation that her daughter
should be forced to do the bidding of such
a man. But at the recital of Otho's attentions there was an expression in her face
which Ada did not interpret as one of
displeasure.

By Mr. Dixon's orders the young
woman had received her betrothed with
outward friendliness, though she declined
with quiet, persistent obstinacy, to say she
was sorry for what had happened. Recon-
ciliations made to order are apt to carry
about them a very strong flavour of their
artificial nature and origin, and this particular reconciliation bore the stamp of
unreality very plainly to be read.

On going in on Christmas Eve, Roger was, for once, not at all sorry to find that the Dixons had friends with them. Mr. Dixon received him heartily, Ada demurely, Mrs. Dixon coldly, scarcely speaking to him at all. There was a miserable constraint and unreality about everything. Roger felt it a relief to himself, and had a bitter conviction that it was also one to Ada, when he had to tell her that he had promised Mr. Johnson to take all the organist's duty on the following day, in order that that official might take a holiday and visit some friends. His time would, therefore, be so much taken up that he would not be able to call and see her before service. She heard his excuse with indifference, and Roger went to bed that night, and arose also on the following morning, with a heavy problem agitating his mind. How was he to treat her? What was he to do with this wilful creature whom he loved so much, and who had

succeeded in making their mutual relations
so miserable and so embarrassed ? For
it was he who had been sinned against,
as he very well knew, and though in his
tenderness he was ready to condone that,
and would have eagerly made an effort
after any reconciliation that should have
reality in it, yet the sense of duty and of
the fitness of things stepped in, and told
him that to let a condition of things be
initiated in which the woman was to be
humoured even when wrong, and the man
was to beg forgiveness for all misunder-
standings, whether caused by himself or not,
was simple madness.   Yet how he was to
institute anything more reasonable, he did
not see, unless Ada were brought to see
that she had behaved badly, of which truth
not the most glimmering consciousness
seemed to have been afforded her.

With this trouble in his mind he went
to church on Christmas morning, and tried,
almost unconsciously, to find a solution to

his difficulties in the language spoken to him by his music. To a certain extent he found what he wanted ; he received sooth-ing, and that alone was a help to counsel. It was not the first time that music had come to him with healing on her wings ; most likely it would not be the last.

Seated up in the organ-loft, and looking into the mirror in front of him, he could see, not only the vicar and his curate, but a good many of the congregation too,—all diminished, reversed in position, moving up and down silently, rising and sitting down again like automata or dream-crea-tures. His sight was keen and long. He could identify a good many of those who came in, and amongst them he saw Ada and her father and mother. Ada, he per-ceived, was not so prostrate under the shock of their quarrel as to have neglected the claims of Christmas Day to be con-sidered a *fête* day in matters of toilette. She was dressed gaily, and he saw a pretty

face, looking prettier still in the framework
of a smart and becoming new bonnet.   It
was a fresh, sweet face, seen thus in repose,
and at a distance, and his heart yearned
towards its owner, and he tried to put out
of his mind the ugly recollection of the
same face turned upwards towards Otho
Askam, with a smile, and afterwards looking at him, cross, distorted, pouting.

Whether the music inspired him, or the
sight of Ada, he knew not, but there
flashed suddenly into his mind the recollection that he must most likely soon lose
sight of her, for a considerable time, at
any rate, and with this recollection the
conviction that that was the best thing
that could possibly happen to them both.
Separation for a season would, he argued,
teach them both to look upon things with
less prejudiced eyes.   She would miss him,
and want him, and he would learn to be
less indignant at what had happened between them.

As he came to this conclusion, which he hugged as a conviction, because it presented to him a way out of his difficulty with regard to the most judicious course to take with Ada, he perceived Gilbert Langstroth walking up the aisle behind Eleanor Askam, and they went together to the great square pew belonging to Thorsgarth. Roger began to wonder if Michael was right in thinking there might be something between them. Then he saw the choir and parsons coming in, and he wound up his voluntary, and the service began. When it was over, he played the congregation out to the music of a quick movement from a sonata of Beethoven—a passage full of storm and stress; of pain, struggle, and striving. And as the wild and noble music pealed out, some of his pain and unrest passed away with it.

When he had left the church, and got into the churchyard, it was almost empty.

One or two groups still lingered in conversation. Ada and her parents were not
amongst them, but Roger was surprised
to see Gilbert and Miss Askam still there.
She looked very pale, he noticed, and
grave, but also very beautiful, in her dark
brown velvet and furs. He raised his hat,
and was passing on, but Gilbert stepped
forward, and to Roger's bewildered amaze-
ment, accosted him.

"I have been waiting for you," said he.
"I want a word with you, if you can spare
a moment; and Miss Askam desires me
to present you to her;" and he turned
from one to the other.   •

Again Roger's hat came off, and he
could not find it in his heart to look with
anything but gentleness upon this sad
young face, in which he, like Michael, had
begun to perceive a nobility and firmness
of expression beneath the mere beauty of
outline, which expression attracted him
whether he would or no. She only said

a very few words to him, quietly and simply.

"I wished to make your acquaintance. I have heard much about you from Dr. Rowntree, and from my friend, Mrs. Johnson."

To which Roger gravely replied that he was highly honoured, and had heard also of Miss Askam from the same friends. He perfectly appreciated the spirit which dictated this advance from her.

"She would repair the wrong, if she could. Poor thing! She might as well try to sweep back the ocean with a besom."

Then Gilbert said to him, "I had no opportunity of speaking to you the other morning, but I want to do so particularly. I have business to discuss with you. Will you meet me to-morrow morning in the reading-room in the town—say at twelve, or earlier if you like?"

"Certainly. Twelve will suit me perfectly. It will no doubt be better that we should have a little talk."

"Thank you.   I shall be punctual," said
Gilbert, with the air of a man who is much
obliged.

They parted, and Roger took his way
to Mr. Dixon's, where he had been bidden
some time ago, to dine and spend the day;
not because he felt any sudden desire for
their society, or they for his, but because
it was Christmas, and it is the proper
thing to go and make merry with your
friends and relations at that season.   He
had to go out once more to play at the
evening service, except for which interval
he spent most of his time in the company
of his betrothed and her parents, with what
results may be imagined.   Ada was no
more gracious, no more penitent to-day,
than she had been yesterday.   Roger's
conviction that a temporary separation
would be good for the spiritual welfare of
both became stronger.   He imparted his
idea to Mr. Dixon, in a private conversation with him, stating his reasons, and

Mr. Dixon entirely agreed with him.
They both brought heavy broadsides of
common sense to bear upon the question,
and neither of them could do more ;
neither of them could have understood, if
some scatter-brained person had stepped
forward, and assured them that to settle a
question of that kind it was most desirable
that to common sense should be joined a
little of the much rarer and more precious
quality of imagination. They saw facts,
and they grappled with them in the very
best way in which they knew how ; and
they were at one in the opinion that Ada,
if left to herself a little, might come to a
better mind.

On the following day, at noon, punctual
to his appointment, Roger repaired to the
reading-room in the town. There was no
one there ; it was holiday time, and people
were otherwise amusing themselves. As
he waited for Gilbert he could not but
reflect how it was they came to meet thus.

"He knows I wouldn't set any foot inside Thorsgarth, and he knows, too, that he need never again darken the door of his brother; so we have to sneak into a public room, where there is neutral ground. It is an odious state of things, and I shall be glad to be out of it."

He had not long to wait. Gilbert arrived directly afterwards, and looked pleased to see him.

"I am much obliged to you for coming," began Gilbert. "It gives me hopes that I shall be successful in my errand."

"I thought you would want to know how the books stand, and so on, ₊for the benefit of my successor, when he arrives."

"Of course that will be necessary, but it is not what I came about to-day. I won't waste words in telling you how annoyed, and more than annoyed I have been—I may say mortified and disgusted, at what has just taken place. I know the value of your services, and that this is no fitting recompense for them."

" I don't know about the value of my services, but I feel as if I had been rubbed the wrong way, and that by no means gently," said Roger.

" Of course. And you will naturally be unwilling to remain without a situation longer than is necessary."

" Naturally. I have done nothing about it yet, because nobody wants to hear about such things at Christmas-time ; but I thought of advertising, or perhaps writing to my former employers directly."

" Yes, of course you could do that. But I have it on my conscience that it was to oblige me and to do me a service that you left those former employers, and it must be my business not to let you suffer for that."

" You are very kind," said Roger, perfectly appreciating the unusual nature of this long memory. " Very kind, you are ;

but I don't see how any one could hold
you responsible for what has happened, or
consider it your fault if a man whom I
have had to do with is such a blackguard,
and shows his blackguardism in such an
offensive manner that I have to leave him.
I've had my wages for more than six years,
and—— "

"You have done a great deal more than
that. You have stuck to the affair from
the beginning, and worked it through good
and bad, till from a doubtful venture you
have made it into a profitable business.
Any common foreman might have stayed
in his place and taken his wages. You
have been something different.   But there
is no need to beat about the bush.   I have
a proposal to make to you.   I have had a
fair measure of success in the business in
which I am engaged.   I think of finally
settling accounts with Mr. Askam, who
has never cared for business of that kind.
I shall pay him the remainder of the

capital and interest still owing to him, and continue to work the mills on my own account; and I thought that under those circumstances you might consent to remain, since you would have the entire management of the concern, and of course a share in the profits, and would have absolutely nothing further to do with Otho Askam. What do you say to it?"

The proposition took Roger by surprise, and embarrassed him at the same time, for it made his decision concerning the separation of Ada and himself seem less than before the only reasonable one to come to. But he was not a man who came to such decisions in a moment of carelessness or impatience, and, having once arrived at them he was hard to move. At first there was a strong feeling of temptation, —the sensation that Gilbert's proposal put an end to all difficulties, and made his way clear before him. This, which was the natural feeling, he immediately began to distrust, chiefly because of his previous resolution to leave Bradstane, and after a few moments of rapid thought decided that to make things clear and right between him and Ada, he would make any sacrifice ; and if this was the sacrifice required—the giving up of this opening— why, the more promptly and rapidly it was accomplished the better.

"This is what I never expected," he at last said slowly, "and it is very tempting."

"That means, that it does not tempt you, but the reverse ; is it not so ?"

"No ; it does tempt me very much. But there are private reasons—reasons which I can't quite explain to you, which I am afraid will prevent it."

"If you say that, I suppose I must not press you. But I am very sorry, if you think you cannot do as I wish. There are several reasons why I wished it very much, apart from the one that you are far better suited to the post than any one else I could possibly find. One is, that if you had accepted, there would have been no further settlements required, since I know you so well ;—no question of references, or recommendations from other persons."

" Yes, I understand that."

" But, if you do not come to me, but take another situation, you will have to refer to your former employer, who, in name, at any rate, has been Mr. Askam."

" Well, and what can Mr. Askam say of me that is not creditable ? "

" Nothing—with truth.　But you are aware that he is unscrupulous and extremely vindictive."

" But there is such a thing as an action for defamation of character, if people tell lies about you.　I have not the slightest fear of any such thing.　He may dislike me, but he is not quite mad, and he simply dare not do it."

"I fear you do not know him so well as I do. 'Daring' has simply nothing to do with it. He is not a man who dares or dares not. He is a creature who yields to every impulse of anger or passion, as blindly and unquestioningly, almost, as when he was a child. He has got an intense hatred for you now, because you have thwarted and spoken plainly to him, and he is now capable of committing any folly in order to punish you. What I wished to say is this, that if you will allow me, I will do all in my power to see you placed as soon as possible in a situation at least as good as the one which, from ho fault of yours, you are forced to leave. And if I am the first to hear of such an opening, I will at once communicate with you ; if you are the first, all I ask of you is, that you will write to me, and not to Mr. Askam, for references. Then I shall be able to see that justice is done, and that no scandal takes place."

Roger yielded to the honest impulse which arose in him, to lay aside all suspicion, and thank Gilbert heartily and unaffectedly.

"I don't pretend it is not a matter of importance to me," he said, "for it is; and I am thankful to be helped forward a bit. I feel very grateful to you."

"You won't take a few days, then, to consider my proposal about the works here?" said Gilbert, looking almost wistfully at him.

Roger shook his head slowly.

"I think it is better not," said he. "I have considered my whole situation carefully since Friday night, and I am perfectly certain that I am best out of Bradstane for a time, both for my own sake, and for that of those most bound up with me. And when I settle down, it would be as well that it should not be here, but somewhere else."

"Very well. I shall not attempt to

alter your decision now. We must see about another situation as speedily as possible."

There was a little pause, during which Roger thought some rather puzzled thoughts. He could not understand Gilbert—that was very natural—and he owned that the character of the other man was a problem to which he had not the key. He felt the charm of manner which years of growth and cultivation had developed in Gilbert, and which is a thing not to be described in so many words. He understood also that Gilbert was acting the part now of a gentleman, an honourable man, and a friend. He gathered that Gilbert disliked and abhorred the conduct of Otho Askam, and his character. That was a group of characteristics which went harmoniously together. What he could not understand, in his simplicity and straightforwardness, was that this same man should still be the friend, adviser, visitor, companion of Askam, whose whole con- duct was so indecent and brutal ; and that in past days he should have descended to the very base intrigue which he had undoubtedly conducted, with regard to the disposal of his father's property. That intrigue, when discovered, had alienated his brother from him for ever ; and, reflected Roger, suddenly, whose money was it with which Gilbert pro- posed to carry on the working of the Townend Mills ? There had never been a word said about the two thousand pounds which Michael had rejected, but which Gilbert had probably manipulated all these years. This wonder started up suddenly in his mind, and with all his disposition to think well of the man who was so readily and so ungrudgingly stepping to his aid, Roger could not stifle those other voices, which spoke of another phase in the said man's character.

His thoughts on the subject, though this was the drift of them, were not thus orderly and formulated. They ran vaguely and ramblingly through his mind, in and out of one another, uncertain and shapeless.

Suddenly Gilbert observed—

" I was present at the concert in the schoolroom the other night, and I saw what happened there."

" Ay ; along with the rest of the world," said Roger, writhing under the recollection of it.

" Yes ; and you must excuse me for mentioning it. I feel it a duty, I may say. There is no harm in your leaving Bradstane under the present circumstances ; but there might have been, but for something that has taken place since the concert. But for this, I should have told you plainly, as a friend, that you would do foolishly to go away, and leave your *fiancée* exposed to the possibility of receiving further attentions from Otho Askam. It would have been by no means an impossible contingency. Now, I am glad to say, there is no danger of it."

"Indeed; and pray to what fortunate circumstance am I indebted for such immunity?"

"Just to this, that after the concert he saw Miss Wynter home, proposed to her, and was accepted. He had accomplished his purpose of frightening and subduing her, though it seems to me that in order to clinch his victory he had to go further than he intended."

"She has got him at last, then," said Roger with contempt. "And now I think of it, that will be an advantage to me, for she can never have anything more to say to my little girl, and there will be an end to an intimacy which I have always detested."

"Yes, you are right to be glad of that.

Hers is not a friendship I should desire
for any woman in whom I was interested."

"The wicked always gain their ends,'
said Roger unguardedly. "I did hope
she would never succeed in catching him,
so far as I hoped anything about it."

"She is not so fortunate, even from
her point of view, as you suppose," said
Gilbert tranquilly. "She has certainly
got what she aimed at, but sadly deteriorated from what it was when she first
began to scheme for it; and with it she
has got a lot of other things thrown in,
which she could well have dispensed
with. If she were any one else I should
feel sorry for her."

"You say that what she schemed for
is deteriorated; now, excuse my saying
it, but how is it that you too cling to
that man? That is a thing which I have
been wondering ever since you came here
this year."

Gilbert's face changed a little.

"I suppose it must be unaccountable
to many another, as well as to you," he
said. "I can only say that it is because
he was true to me, in his way, long ago,
when I had other hopes and other am-
bitions than I have now. He was not
afraid to declare that he was my friend,
and that whoever spoke against me, insulted him. It would conduce greatly to
my comfort and peace of mind, if I could
forget that; but I cannot. So my relations to him are defined, not by my
present opinion of him, but by his conduct towards me in former days. Other
things happened at that time; I know it
is useless to speak to you of it, but he
stood my friend when no one else would
have done. Otho Askam is my Old Man
of the Sea. We all have one of some
kind, and it seems to me that the best
thing to do with them is to carry them
quietly as long as one's strength holds
out."

" You say it is useless to speak to me
of that past time. But, since we have
got so far below the surface in our talk,
there is one thing I would like to tell
you, without any prejudice to my friendship with Michael. You sent a note to
him one day."

" Yes."

" He gave it to me to read at the time."

" Yes ? "

" I urged him to take a day to consider
the matter, and I have always felt that
you were wronged by his refusing to do
so. But his own wrongs at that time
were so incomparably greater than yours,
and his heart was so broken, that I have
always condoned the fault, though I was
sorry for it.   Now you know all."

" I am glad you have told me. His
heart was so broken, you say," said Gilbert, speaking with an evident effort. " I
did not dare to think of anything connected with him, then. He—is he—do

you think it would be a breach of confidence to let me know something of his
circumstances ? "

" I am afraid he would think so. He
does not even know I am meeting you."

" Ah ! Say nothing then. But—his
engagement with Miss Wynter. Surely
he cannot regret now that it was broken
off ? "

" I don't suppose he does. That did
not make the blow at the time less hard."

" No, no ! I should have fancied somehow that he would have married some one
else. But he has not."

" No, he has not."

" Do you think he has ever cared to ? "

" He never had, up to a little while
ago."

" And now you think he does ? "

" No, I don't. I think he has been so
well-disciplined by what he has gone
through that it would take a great deal
to make him really want to marry any

one. He can't help admiring beautiful things, but he won't do anything so disastrous as to fall in love with the lady I am thinking of. And besides, I know nothing about his feelings, really. He does not wear his heart upon his sleeve— now."

"No. Of course I look upon all this as said in confidence ; and I think that for the present we have settled all we had to do."

"Yes, quite, I think. And I assure you I am much obliged to you."

"Not at all. I am glad to have had the talk. You have my London address, I think."

"Yes. How long do you remain here ? "

"Only a few days more."

They exchanged good mornings, and separated. Roger, going home, was very thoughtful. He knew he had taken a momentous step in refusing to remain in

Bradstane. He believed it was the best step that was open to him, and he took it. It is what men have to do on their way through life. Steps of some kind we have to take, though each one may be fraught with consequences which we cannot foresee, and which we can only appreciate after we have lost all power in the matter. We can look on, in these after days, at the results of our actions ; it is permitted to us to rejoice in the fruits of our conduct, or, as often as not, to repine over the same, or to beat our breasts and wish we had never been born, —but not to alter by so much as a hair's-breadth, the direction of the road opened out long ago by our own deed.

CHAPTER II.

SERMON, BY A SINNER.

GILBERT had said to Roger that he was
only remaining a few days longer at
Thorsgarth; but as a matter of fact, he
stayed till over the New Year,—being
able, seemingly, to put off the business
which, he every now and then remarked
in a casual way, called aloud to him from
London. He could hardly have enjoyed
himself much, during the latter portion
of his visit—at least, that was Eleanor's
feeling, as she uneasily watched the course
of events after the concert. For a few
days she was quite in the dark as to the
exact state of things. Of course she lay

awake a long time on that particular
night, feeling uneasy about every subject
to which her thoughts turned,—Otho, Gilbert, Magdalen, Ada ; she felt no sense
of security or comprehension with regard
to any one of them. Why did Magdalen,
after behaving so well at first under the
insult which Otho had put upon her, fall
off so lamentably afterwards—tamely sub-
mitting to his behest, and allowing him to
drive home with her ?

And Gilbert—in whom, to a certain
extent, she had put her trust—was no more
than a broken reed. He had promised to
see that all should go right, and, on the
contrary, everything had gone wrong—
just as wrong as it could possibly go ;
and he seemed neither vexed nor uneasy
about it, but allowed things to take their
course.

When she met Otho at lunch, after his
quarrel with Roger, and saw his sullen
look, and heard his sulky, curt remarks

and replies, she felt miserable, in spite
of telling herself that it was no affair of
hers ; and she did not venture to inquire
what had angered him. She vaguely
dreaded to hear his reply. The Christmas Day, which happened also to be a
Sunday, came ; and the doctor's Christ-
mas-tree was to be on the twenty-sixth.
She had not seen Mrs. Johnson since the
concert, and was therefore in ignorance
as to what had happened at the mills, and
it suited Gilbert for a day or two to say
nothing to her. So she lived on in uneasiness, and sometimes caught herself
thinking of her former life, which she had
left six weeks ago, as if it were a hundred
years away from her ; and of her uncle
and cousin Paul on their travels, as if they
were inhabitants of another world, journey-
ing on seas and in lands unheard of.

Things were in this condition on Monday
afternoon, and she was sitting alone in her
parlour in the waning daylight, when Bar-

low came in with a message from Gilbert, to know if she would see him. Her thoughts, which had strayed away from the painful present, were suddenly pulled back again to their post. Instinctively bracing herself to meet something disagreeable, she bade Barlow show Mr. Langstroth up, and then sat and waited for him.

In a minute, however, he was with her; and, as usual, his presence, unwished for, and even dreaded in anticipation, proved in reality soothing, almost agreeable. Eleanor struggled against this power of Gilbert to make himself agreeable to her; resented it deeply in her heart, as a sort of disloyalty to his brother, to whom she had in her soul given irrevocably and for ever, the place of master of her heart and destiny. This last was as strong a feeling as anything which could be experienced; but, nevertheless, Gilbert possessed this power of being agreeable to her when he came, and the fact puzzled and annoyed her more than she would have cared to own.

"You are very kind to let me see you," he said at once, as he took the chair she pointed to. "I have been wanting to speak to you for a day or two—about Otho."

"Ah, I knew it was about Otho. Say on, and let us have done with it."

"Perhaps that will not be so easy, either. However, I will say on, as you suggest. Before I could speak to you, I wished to accomplish a certain piece of business. I have now done so, and am free to say what I like. I suppose you have been noticing how angry Otho looks, without being able in your own mind to assign a cause for it?"

"Unless the cause is that he is unhappy because he has been doing wrong."

Gilbert repressed a smile.

"I am afraid I cannot comfort you by confirming that theory of yours. By 'doing wrong,' I suppose you mean his little escapade at the concert the other night. Yes, I see. Well, I imagine he has forgotten all about that by now. He is angry, or 'unhappy,' if you like, because he has been, and is being, put to great inconvenience, and he doesn't like it; it makes him uncomfortable."

Then he told her about the quarrel between Otho and Roger, with a sort of amused carelessness, as if he had been diverted by the combat, and somewhat contemptuous of the combatants, which tone puzzled and did not reassure his hearer.

"Otho does not like office work," he went on, smiling openly. "He has not had much of it yet; but the factories reopen to-morrow, after the holiday, and then he will have to try a little of it. I have telegraphed to a man whom I know to send down some one suitable, and I have promised Otho to wait until the some one comes, and just to put him in the way of business; but it may be a week or so before my friend can hit upon the right kind of man. That makes him very angry——"

"You don't seem to think anything of the way in which *he* has behaved," burst forth Eleanor indignantly, and the colour high in her cheeks. "I think it is the most abominable thing I ever heard of—his treating Mr. Camm in that way. It is—it is ——"

Words failed her. She felt as if she would choke with anger and disgust. Gilbert's eyes were fixed upon her face; the slight smile was still hovering about his lips.

"You talk about what makes *him* angry, as if it mattered. He deserves to be put to inconvenience. He does not deserve to be helped out of it. What becomes of Mr. Camm?"

"Oh, I have seen Roger. We understand each other. But don't you want to hear all that I have to tell you? I have another piece of news."

"What is it?" she asked, feeling from the way in which he spoke that it must be news of some importance, and staying her anger to hear it.

"Something else has happened, which ought to have made him forget his anger, one would think. I told him he ought to tell you about it, but he says he won't; it is all between him and her. He does not feel inclined to talk about it, and, in short, I see you half guess already. Yes; it is quite true. He got engaged to Miss Wynter the other night."

"Engaged — to — Miss — Wynter!" Eleanor stared at him incredulously. "She took him—after what he had done?"

Gilbert laughed aloud.

"She took him, it would appear. I thought you ought to be informed of it. Probably all the neighbourhood is gossiping over it by now, and you would have looked ridiculous if you had heard people talking about it, and had not understood."

" I—oh, to be ridiculous is nothing, it seems to me, if one is not disgraceful," said Eleanor, and paused, because she could not help wondering what Gilbert felt about it himself. If she were to judge from his present manner, she would have said that he regarded it all from a superior stand-point, as a kind of joke amongst some unsophisticated creatures, whose habits it amused him to study ; but, recollecting the very different tone he had lately taken, and his present avowed conviction that he thought it serious enough to come and tell her about it, since Otho would not, she felt that his motives were quite beyond her comprehension. So she ceased to specu-late upon them, and turned her attention to another point.

" It is all very extraordinary to me, and most disagreeable—the way in which it has been done," she said, and again caught the

curious expression, half amusement, half—
what? in Gilbert's look. "You know
them both much better than I do. Do
you think it will be for his good?"

"In a way, I am sure it will. It is perfectly certain that whatever kind of woman
Miss Wynter may be, as a woman, she is
the only one who has, or ever had, any
shadow of influence over him. She knows
him thoroughly. She knows the frightful
risks she is running,—perhaps she does not
feel them frightful—and she knows the
precarious state of his fortunes at the
present time. With her eyes open she
has taken him. If they would or could be
married at once she might do a great deal
to retrieve his affairs."

"I did not mean that exactly," said
Eleanor, going on with what she did mean,
despite what seemed to her Gilbert's look
of mockery. "I was thinking more of the
moral influence. I should have thought
that a woman of higher mind — one

who would have roused him to better
things——"

"Yes, that is a very fine idea," said
Gilbert, with ready benevolence—" that
theory of overcoming evil with good.
The thing is, how far is it practicable?
You speak as a woman, and a good woman.
I see as a man, and a man of the world.
And speaking from my knowledge of men
in general, and of your brother Otho in
particular, I should say Miss Wynter
would make him a far more suitable wife
than the best of women, filled with high
aspirations and noble aims. Magdalen
Wynter understands him by reason of
being composed of a similar clay. Understanding him, she will lead him—at
least, very often. A saint would simply
exasperate him into something ten times
worse than he is. You do not know the
ease, the comfort, and the help it is to be
understood ; how it can keep a wavering
man in the right, and drag a sinning man

out of the wrong. Good people don't need half as much understanding as bad ones, and with due respect to you and to current notions on the subject, saints and people who never do wrong are not those who are the most sympathetic and comprehending. It sounds very degrading, I dare say, but it is true—true as anything can be."

Gilbert spoke with much more emphasis than usual, and with a shade of bitterness in his tone. Had Roger Camm been there, he would have understood it in a moment; it would have confirmed some vague suspicions long entertained by him. But to Eleanor, it seemed as if Gilbert were composing an apology for wrongdoing; making it out as being rather meritorious than otherwise. With emphasis equal to his own, and with some bitterness in her tone also, she replied—

" I dare say you may be right. Men of the world usually are right, on the outside,

at any rate; but I look inside, and it seems
to me that all this is very sad and dreadful,
too. Life is full of these horrible con-
tradictions, and it appears as if you can
never have any good or beautiful thing
without as it were a heap of dust and
ashes beside it, spoiling it all."

Gilbert laughed a little, and she felt
chilled—not vexed with him—as she was
conscious she ought to have been, but dis-
couraged by the fact that he was about to
differ from her.

"Why, of course," he admitted. "Is it
not in the very nature of life, as we know
life, that it should be so? What are the
good and beautiful things, as you call
them, except sacrifices and aspirations or
struggles after something higher and better
than our everyday fight and grind? And
how can you have beautiful sacrifices without something bad and mean to call them
out? and how can you aspire after the
better, without a worse which makes the

better desirable to you ? But for the dust-heaps, I do not really see how the shrines and temples would ever get their due share of admiration."

"Admiration !" repeated Eleanor indignantly ; "as if one *admired* a holy place ! I dare say you have risen superior to all such superstitious considerations, but I say again, I think it is horrible ; and I maintain that I do not think Miss Wynter is a good or a high-principled woman, and I am very sorry Otho is going to marry her."

"Which of them do you look upon as the temple, and which as the cinder-heap ?" asked Gilbert politely, but with a queer look. Eleanor was furious with herself for laughing out, quickly and readily ; but she had to admit that Gilbert had the best of it. Then a sudden gravity came over her ; she caught her breath, and looked at him in renewed bewilderment. In what light did he wish her to see him ; how did he desire her to view him, that he, who had cheated his brother, and undermined his father's integrity, should have the effrontery to sit there and talk lightly about wrong being necessary to call forth the higher life, and to say that temples could not be properly "admired," unless there were sordid details close to them, to emphasize their beauty? Seen from her point of view, his conversation was sickening in its hypocrisy and unreality; and yet —again the feeling of surprise came over her—she was interested in it; she could not feel revolted. Was the man's personal influence really so potent as to nullify all the effect of what she knew to his disadvantage?

Gilbert had listened to her last words with an amused smile, betraying by nothing whether she hurt him or not; his gaze met hers steadily, and he continued to watch her while she silently reflected. At last he said, lightly still, and coldly—

"I see you are wondering what to make

of me. It is very natural—in you ; and if you can trust me far enough to believe that anything disinterested can proceed out of my mouth, I would suggest to you not to go on wondering any more, but to listen to me, and attentively consider what I have to say to you."

Eleanor started, reddening with confusion, and feeling, with a sudden revulsion, as some child might, which, instead of attending to its professor's discourse, had been speculating about the wrinkles on the brow of the learned man, and was suddenly called to order. An immense distance seemed to open up at once between her and Gilbert. She remembered the sentiments she had attributed to him of admiration for herself, and felt that egregious vanity must have led her very far astray.

" Indeed, I will listen to whatever you have to say. I think you are very kind to take so much trouble about—poor Otho."

" 'Poor Otho,' as you call him, is my

oldest friend; I know him better than any
one else does, except perhaps the lady we
have been speaking of, whose acquaintance
with him dates from the very same time.
You laughed just now—you could not help.
Does not your common sense now explain
to you that it is much better to take men
as they are, and provide them with the
best that circumstances will allow, instead
of wanting to insist on their having for
mate an ideal which does not suit, and
which they would hate if they had to live
with it?   That is my view of the case."

"Very well," said she resignedly. "Go
on."

"I was about to observe that though
Otho certainly appears disposed just now
to kick over the traces altogether, and not
listen to anything that any one has to say
to him, yet I think I may still say, I have
more influence over him than any one else
has. But upon my soul, I do not know
how long it may last. He has got some

notion into his head which, for a wonder, he has not confided to me, and I cannot answer for the freaks which it may inspire him to play. I wonder if you will think me impertinent for asking, did you know much about Otho and his character before you came to live here?"

"No—at least, my uncle, Mr. Stanley, used to say he was afraid Otho was rather fast, and told me not to let him bet. I think," added Eleanor, with rather a sad smile, "that if we had known him better, we should not have wasted our words in that way."

"I think something still more probable is, that you would not have wasted your time in coming here."

"I did not choose to come here. It so fell out that this was the right place for me to come to."

"You had nowhere else to go?"

"Practically nowhere. My aunt died, and my uncle's health had so given way

that he and Paul—my cousin, and their only
child—have gone to travel together for an
indefinite time.   Where should I have
thought of coming to but to my *home?*"

She raised her head, and looked at him
both proudly and sadly.   Gilbert's eyes
fell—not in confusion, but reflectively.

"True," he admitted after a moment.
"And you intend to remain here?"

"Certainly I do.   Why should I go?"

"Oh, there are many reasons.   It is not
a pleasant house for you to be in."

Eleanor felt as if Otho's conduct were
being commented upon, and she herself
tutored by some one who was much more
master of the situation than she was.   She
did not exactly like it, but she was powerless to resent it; she did not quite know
whether she wished even to resent it.

"It is a dreary house," said she at
length.   "It is depressing to me, too.
But I don't know that one may always
leave a place just because it happens not
to be pleasant."

"Ah! You know Otho is going away when I do?"

"Yes."

"I will answer for it that you will not see much more of him till after the Derby Day, and perhaps not then. Don't you think it would be advisable for you to have a change, too?"

"A change—in the depth of winter—after being here just six weeks? No, I do not."

"You are very decided, I see. Pardon me for pressing the question again. Are you quite decided to stay here?"

"Yes. Why not? Why should I go away? It is my home, as I said before," she said, looking at him rather impatiently.

"You will be very dull. Otho, you see, has no scruples about leaving you, and will not return an hour the sooner from the knowledge that you are here alone."

"And if I like Bradstane, and wish to

remain at Thorsgarth, in spite of this dulness, and in spite of what Otho does?"

He shrugged his shoulders.

"Of course, in that case. There are compensations sometimes, which go a long way towards repaying a little dulness and solitude. Every one to his taste. If that is yours, I may as well proceed to tell you that my advice to you would be to prepare for reverses."

"Reverses?"

"Yes. Racing, and the sort of horse dealing in which Otho indulges—never to mention a dozen other expensive little trifles that he likes, are not profitable occupations, and he has not found them so. I speak plainly. You may live to see very evil days at Thorsgarth, if you choose to remain here. You may live to see Otho reduced to poverty, and, if your feelings are easily worked upon, your own fortune in danger—that is, if you should let yourself be deluded into the idea that you can help him out of his difficulties, and set him on his legs again."

"I think I could meet reverses, if they came, without too much lamenting."

"In addition to which he may at any time get married to your favourite, Magdalen Wynter, and request you to find another home."

"I have a house of my own, and I should not wait to be asked to go."

"Oh, you mean the Dower House—a nice old house, that. It stands quite near to my own old home, the Red Gables."

"Yes. I have thought sometimes it would be a pleasant house to live in, as—— "

"As you are so much alone," interposed Gilbert almost eagerly. "Don't you really think that it would be much better than for you to be here, alone, without chaperon or companion—— "

"Nay," interposed Eleanor, half-smiling ; "don't twit me with that. I don't want a chaperon ; but if I did, how could I have one, when you know very well that Otho says—— "

She stopped.   Otho had said that one petticoat in the house was more than enough for him, and he would put up with no more.   Gilbert smiled.

" Yes, I know what Otho says.   I was not twitting you.   I only wish you would see that reason tells you to leave him, and not mix yourself in his affairs."

" Your reason may.   Mine does not. Mine tells me that Otho is my brother ; and I'm sure he is wretched with his own wrong doing, though you scoff at the idea. Do you mean to tell me that Otho is happy ?—you cannot.   And my reason tells me that, sometime, I might find a way of helping him.   He might want to come home and have some one to be kind to him, sometime.   And I might be away, and never hear of it till a long time afterwards.   I don't mean to say that nothing would induce me ever to go to the Dower House; that is a different thing. But I will not think of leaving Bradstane. Men's reason is proverbially superior to women's reason, you know. Perhaps that is why we don't agree."

"Perhaps it is," said he tranquilly. "After what you have said it would be impertinence in me to urge anything further. Perhaps I have gone too far already. I was under the impression that you were very unhappy in Bradstane, but I am pleased to find that my fears were exaggerated. I am very glad you have found mitigating circumstances, and I hope the good may continue to outweigh the evil in your estimation."

He spoke politely and coldly. Eleanor sat silent and almost breathless. Gilbert had never spoken to her thus before. She was alarmed at his tone, and it brought back to her recollection all the dissertations she had heard from Dr. Rowntree on the

subject of his infernal cleverness, as the
worthy Friend called it. At the same
moment she recalled a descriptive sentence
which she had heard Otho utter not long
ago. "Finding"—he had said, speaking
of some acquaintance who had long un-
successfully wooed a lady—"finding the
sentimental dodge no go, he took to in-
timidation, and fairly bullied her into it."

A convulsive smile twitched her lips.
She did not believe now that Gilbert's
altered tone arose from disappointed sentiment. A much more prosaic reason
suggested itself to her, namely, that the
sentiment had been assumed in order to
amuse himself, and see what the effect
would be upon her. He must stand sorely
in need of some kind of amusement at
Thorsgarth, she reflected, and that was
the one nearest to his hand. His present
demeanour and sentiments were probably
those of the natural man. What he had
just said convinced her that he did not

more than half believe in her desire to remain in order to be of some possible service to Otho. She was more than ever sure of this when he rose and said—

" I will not detain you any longer, I know you are going out this evening, and I know that children's parties begin early, as a rule."

" Yes, that is——— "

"Oh, I know what a benevolent old gentleman Dr. Rowntree is, especially to those who are his favourites. He would like to give them all Christmas presents and kisses, young and old, big and little. I wish you a very pleasant evening."

She was silent still. Gilbert wished her good afternoon, and departed.

From various allusions which he let fall before he went away, he gave her to understand that he knew Michael had been at the doctor's party. Eleanor tried to ignore these hints, and to look openly at Gilbert when he spoke of his brother;

but her heart was hot within her, with
mingled fear and indignation; fear lest
he should even yet harbour some scheme
of harm against Michael; indignation at
what she considered his audacity in
naming him, and a miserable sense that
she had better not provoke him, or the
results might be bad for Otho. Gilbert
sought her society no more; he had no
more of those pleasant, gentle . things
to say to her, such as he had uttered
on the night of the concert. She became
convinced that he regarded her with
dislike, if not with enmity, and she with-
drew herself as much as possible from his
and Otho's society. Gilbert had yet
another twist to give to the tangled coil
into which her thoughts had got, concerning him, and he did it ingeniously. He
was alone with her in the drawing-room,
after dinner, on the evening before the
day on which he and Otho were to depart

He took a card case from his pocket,

extracted a card from it, and gave it to her.

"That is my London address," said he, with the blandest of smiles. "If you should ever—since you will remain at Thorsgarth — find yourself involved in difficulties with Otho, or in any other circumstances in which the advice of a— business man would be of any use to you, telegraph there to me, and I will be with you within four-and-twenty hours."

"Oh, Mr. Langstroth—— "

"Don't, pray, trouble yourself to express any gratitude. How do you know what dark motives may lurk beneath my seeming kindness? We leave by the seven thirty train in the morning, so I shall not be likely to see you again. I will therefore wish you good-bye now."

"Good-bye," said she hesitatingly, feeling as if she ought to add something to the baldness of the word, but utterly at a loss to know what that something should be.

"I shall, I hope, be here again for the shooting, if not before," said Gilbert. "I shall hope to find you well, and as pleased with Thorsgarth—and Bradstane, too—as you are now."

With which he left her, with his words, and the tone of them, echoing in her ears, and with the shadow of his shadowy smile floating still before her eyes. She was as far as ever from being able to decide whether he was a gross hypocrite, or only a man who had once done very wrong, and was now trying to do very right. That he might be something between the two did not occur to her.   •

CHAPTER III.

BRASS POTS AND EARTHENWARE PIPKINS.

THE worst of winter had stormed itself
away, and it was March—the latter end
of March. The leonine portion of his
reign had endured a long time this year,
and though it was now over, the warmer
gales had yet some north-east to blow
back, and the dominion of the lamb had
not fairly set in. And yet, there was the
caress of spring in the air—that caress
which is unmistakable, and which may be
felt, if it be there, through the bleakest
wind and the coldest rain. This caress
was in the air, and the hue of spring was
in the sky. Here and there her fingers

had swept aside the withered leaves, and allowed a violet to push its way up; and in some very sheltered southern corners appeared a tuft or two of primroses. In the garden borders at Thorsgarth, the crocuses were beginning to make a gallant show. The blue behind the rolling white clouds was deep and profound, — steady and to be relied upon. In the shady corners of the garden, under the budding trees, the clumps of daffodils were putting forth their tender first shoots, ready to nod their heads and laugh through the April showers. And the grass, too, was recovering its colour,— its green, which weeks under the snow had faded and browned. · Everything was full of promise. Nature stepped forward, erect and laughing, jocund, casting the burden of her sadness behind her; not as in autumn, advancing droopingly towards it.

So much for the garden, the cultivated.

Outside, the roads were heavy and soft
with mud; but it was a mud to make glad
the heart of man, especially farming man.
The ploughed fields, stretching their great
shoulders towards the uplands, looked rich
in their purple-brown hue. The hedge-
rows here and there seemed to wear a
filmy, downy veil, the first output of
yellow-green buds. In the great pastures
near Rookswood, on the Durham side of
Tees, the giant ash trees stood yet in
their winter bareness, giving no sign, save
by the hard, burnished black buds, which
for months to come were meaning to hold
fast their secret wealth of bud and leaf,
their treasure of summer glory. There
was every promise that this year the oak
would be out before the ash, with, it was
to be hoped, the proverbial result.

It was on such an afternoon as this,
when the breeze blew from the south-
west, that Eleanor walked along one of
the muddy lanes leading from Thorsgarth

to Bradstane. Beside her trotted Mrs. Johnson's little girl, Effie, whom Eleanor had borrowed a week or two ago from her mother, to keep her company in the solitude of Thorsgarth. For Gilbert's prophecy had been fulfilled. She found it very lonely there, so lonely that she was now on her way, half-willingly, half-reluctantly, to the Dower House, in order to inspect it from garret to cellar, and think whether it would not better suit her as a residence than the great dreary house which had grown so oppressive to her.

As they came in their walk to a bend in the river, Effie suddenly said—

"How full the river is just now; and so brown and strong! Dr. Langstroth says he remembers the river longer than anything else; and he says that Tees is as broad as Bradstane is long. Isn't that queer?"

Eleanor laughed. It is an indubitable fact, and one which she had herself noted with amusement during the first part of her stay in Bradstane, that in a town like this, or, indeed, in any small town or village situated upon a stream as big as the Tees, " the river" becomes the important feature of the neighbourhood. What it looks like, whether it be high or low; in winter, whether the river be frozen or flowing; and in fishing-time, what sort of a water the river shows to-day; whether there has been rain to the north-west, which floods it, or whether drought, which makes it dry. Whenever the conversation turns upon out-of-door subjects, the river is sure to assert itself somewhere or other, and that before very long. It is the same as a living thing, and that a powerful one; its moods are watched and recorded as if they were the moods of a person in whom one took a deep interest. It is for ever the river, the river; and this watery friend, and enemy—for it is both—gives a colour, and has an influence over the lives that are lived near it, which is very remarkable, especially to those who know nothing of such surroundings. And Tees, be it remarked, is a river with a powerful individuality, which none in his vicinity can afford to despise.

"He says that because people think so much about the river here," said Eleanor. "You must know how they talk about it. You never go anywhere without finding the Tees,—in people's houses as well as here flowing through the meadows. That is what he means."

"I suppose it must be," said Effie, who was a philosophical child. And they went on in silence. Eleanor resumed the mental debate which had been occupying her before—as to the wisdom of the step she contemplated taking. It would be separating herself from Otho, at one moment, she thought; and then she remembered Gilbert's dry words—that Otho left her without scruple, and that no thought of her loneliness would bring him back a moment before it was convenient or pleasant to him to come. That was true; she would most likely see quite as much of him at the Dower House as at Thorsgarth. She had not had a line from him since he had gone away with Gilbert to London. Once or twice she had seen Magdalen, who had mentioned having heard from him; but Eleanor suspected that his letters to Magdalen even, were very brief. Miss Wynter volunteered no details or news, and Eleanor felt no more drawn to her than before, and disdained to ask for information which was not proffered.

Once or twice she had ventured on making a tour of inspection all round the Thorsgarth park and grounds, penetrating even to the courtyards, the kennels, and stables which lay behind the house. What she saw there did not tend to encourage her. She found that everything was conducted with a lavish profusion, a reckless extravagance, which would have been foolish in any case ; and it was a lavishness which had also its stingy side, as such lavishness usually has. While necessary repairs were left neglected for months, or undone altogether, many pounds would be spent on some new contrivance for warming or ventilating a stable, already luxuriously fitted up. While some of the men on the farm complained that their carts were falling to pieces, silver-mounted harness was accumulating in the harness-room, for no earthly purpose except to make a show behind the glass doors. Many another extravagant and senseless fancy or whim was indulged to the full, while ordinary necessaries were stinted. It seemed to Eleanor that the establishment swarmed with servants, both men and maids. Their functions and offices were a mystery to her. They always seemed exceedingly busy when she appeared upon the scene, but she had an uneasy consciousness that it was only in seeming, and that as soon as her back was turned, a very different state of things again prevailed. She had been accustomed to a liberal, and even splendid establishment, but one conducted on principles of enlightened economy—without a superfluous retainer, but at the same time without a fault or a failure, from one year's end to the other. The contrast which she saw here offended her sense of decency and order. She knew that Otho ought to retrench, and she would gladly have helped him to do so, with the joy usually brought to bear by women, unskilled in active financial matters, upon this negative process of saving by means of renouncing things.

Thinking over these things, she now walked with Effie towards the Dower House. The old square, when they reached it, looked very pleasant that sunny afternoon; bright sunshine lighting up all the sober, solid old houses, which stood

reposefully, as if secure for ever of peace
and plenty; their quiet closed doors and
shining window panes revealing nothing
of the emotions which might be stirring
those who inhabited them. The trees on
either side the square had begun to show
a first tinge of green, like the rest of
nature. Not a soul stirred in the afternoon quietness; only Michael's great
dog, Pluto, who lay basking on the flags
outside the Red Gables, looked and
blinked at them lazily as they passed,
and slightly moved the tip of his tail in
reply to their greeting. Next door but
one was the Dower House—a pleasant
old stone building, gray, with a door in
the middle, and two windows on either
side; upstairs five windows, and a third
story with five windows more. It was,
in fact, a large, substantial stone house,
very suitable as the country residence of
a single woman of some means and position.
It stood on the sunny side of the square,

and like nearly all the houses in it, its gardens and its pleasantest rooms lay to the back. It was furnished with old-fashioned furniture, and kept in order by an old gardener and his wife, who lived there. Eleanor liked it. She liked the windows looking into the broad open street. Such a prospect seemed to bring her nearer to humanity, and to the wholesome everyday life of her fellow-creatures. The recollection of Thorsgarth, rising stately from its basement of velvet sward, rendered dark by the towering trees which surrounded it,—of the terraces sloping to the river; the flights of steps, the discoloured marble fauns and nymphs—this recollection came over her, and made her feel dreary. She felt as if she had lived in it all for years, and had no joy in any one of them.

In her own mind she almost resolved to go to this other house, but she wished to wait for Otho's return, and explain it all to him—if ever he should return ; if only he would return !

Three days later, without letter and without warning, he came home, late in the evening, having no apologies to make, and very few remarks concerning his long absence and silence. He sat for an hour or two with his sister, and she found something in his looks and aspect which did not tend to allay whatever anxiety she might have felt about him. The ruddy brown of his skin had grown sallow and dark, and his cheeks were hollow. There was a haggard look about him, and the traces, unmistakably to be read, that he had been living hard and fast. His eyes had sunk ; he was not an encouraging spectacle, and there was an uneasy restlessness about him which fretted her. She tried to talk about commonplace things.

" Did you see much of the Websters ? " she asked, alluding to some distant cousins with whom she had been on terms of

intimacy in former days—days which now
seemed very far back.

"Websters—no! When I go to town,
I don't go to do the proper with them. I
have other friends and other places to
go to."

"Lucy told me in a letter that Dick had
met you somewhere."

"And I've met Dick," retorted Otho,
with an uncomplimentary sneer; "and
a precious prig he is."

"Indeed, Otho, he is not. He is a very
nice lad, and very free from priggishness.
That's his great charm."

"He's a young milksop."

"He is neither vulgar nor dissipated,
if that is what you mean."

"I haven't wasted my time in thinking
about him."

"And Mr. Langstroth — how did you
leave him?"

"Gilbert—oh, he's flourishing. By the
way, he sent a message to you,—rather a

complimentary message—and he told me to be sure and not change it into the very reverse of what he wished it to be." Otho chuckled a little. " Let me see. He wished to be remembered to you, sent his best compliments, and hoped to see you again during the year—perhaps when he comes for the shooting. I fancy Gilbert was a bit taken with you, Eleanor. He was mighty particular about his message."

" You fancy very uncalled for things."

" Hey, but I wouldn't mind having him for a brother-in-law," persisted Otho; but he was too careless even to look at her as he aired his views. " A first-rate fellow is Gilbert, and he has rid me of those blessed factories, and stumped up like a man. I've never repented standing his friend when I did."

She made no answer, and as they were alone (for Eleanor had judged it better to send Effie into the background) there was a silence—that profound silence only

to be heard in the country. Suddenly
Otho started, passed his hand over his
eyes, and exclaimed impatiently—

"What a hole of a place this is! What
a deadly stillness; it's enough to give one
the blues. I'd open the window, only that
would make it worse, letting in the 'swish'
of that beastly river, which is a sound I
hate. I do detest the country," he continued, poking the fire with vigour. "Give
me the pavement, and chambers, where
you hear the rattle going on all night.
This confounded place would depress the
spirits of a dog, I do believe."

"Does Magdalen know you are here?
Why don't you go up and see her?"

"Magdalen?" He gave a little start.
"Oh, never mind Magdalen! She understands me. She is not a child, nor a love-
sick girl, to expect me to be always at her
apron-strings. I shall see Magdalen, trust
me. But I'm off into Friarsdale the day
after to-morrow."

" Friarsdale again ! "

" Ay !   There's a heap of things to see after.   I shall have to be back and forward from there till it's time to take Crackpot down to Epsom. . . . Did you ever see a Derby, Eleanor ? "

" No."

" Would you like to ? "

" Not when a horse of yours is running."

" Little   starched   out   puritan !   You might write a tract, or get Michael Langstroth to do it, and have it printed, and salve your conscience over, by distributing it over the grand stand."

" I have something to say to you, Otho. I do not like living alone in this great house when you are so much away ; and I have been thinking whether to go to the Dower House, and take up my abode there."

" Hoh ! " Otho paused.   " While you are about it, why not cut the whole concern, and go to the Websters ? " he said. " They would be overjoyed to have you.

It doesn't suit you ?   I knew it wouldn't ;
but you would come.   You see, my
dear, when a little earthenware pipkin
of a woman jumps into the water, and is
for sailing along with the brass pots, she
generally comes to grief.   My life suits
me ; but it is so unlike all you have been
accustomed to, that you can't fit into it—
can't even settle down to look on at it.
You look downright ill now, and——"

"Otho ! that shows how little you understand," said she, a convulsive laugh struggling with her inner bitterness of heart.
The whole thing came before her as so
tragi-comic ; so horrible, yet so laughable.
So Otho thought that playing fast and
loose with his life, drinking and dicing,
brawling and betting, and generally con-
ducting himself like a blackguard, was a
fine, heroic thing—a proof that he was a
brass pot amongst men, and able to sail
unharmed down *that* stream.   Ludicrous,
pitiable, agonizingly laughable theory !

"It remains to be proved which of us two is the brass pot, and which the pipkin," she went on, unable to help smiling. "For my part, I fancy we are both made of very common clay. But, to leave parables, I would rather not go to the Websters. My ideas about life and other things have changed very much lately. I would rather not return to my old one at present. I should prefer to go to the Dower House, if it will be all the same to you."

"Oh, quite. Since you prefer to stay here. It is an odd taste, I think, for a girl brought up as you have been. But you are better away from here. There's no doubt of that."

Eleanor was looking at him as he spoke, and saw, more plainly than before, the haggardness, and the lines upon his face; it seemed to her that they had been planted there since she had last seen him, but this might be imagination. She was

startled by a resemblance which she
fancied she discovered in this altered face
of his, to a miniature of their father
which was in her possession—that father
who had been in tastes, character, and
disposition, so utterly unlike the son who
followed him. Since coming to Thorsgarth she had often studied this miniature,
wondering how such a father came to
have such a son. At this moment Otho
was leaning his head back, as if weary.
His wild eyes were closed, so that their
strange, savage look did not distort the
likeness. Compunction, longing, yea, love
rushed into her heart.

"Otho!" she said, in a voice which
trembled; and he looked up.

"What's up?" he demanded, seeing
with surprise that she had risen and was
coming towards him.

"Dear Otho!" she repeated, as she
knelt before him, and clasped his hand
in her own; "*why* am I better away from

you ? Why better away from my own
brother, and my father's house, where he
intended me to find my home ? It is
not right, Otho ; it is not right that it
should be so. Ah, if you would only be
different, how happy we might be—you
and Magdalen and I ; and where in all
your world outside will you find anything
that will endure as our love to you will ?—
for I know that Magdalen does love you,
though you treat her cruelly, as you treat
me."

Otho stared down into her face with a
strange, alien glance; a shocked, wondering look. He was not rough ; he did
not repulse her, but he looked as if she
had been apostrophizing him in some
strange tongue, which he could not understand. Presently he said—

" Little girl, you don't know what you
are talking about. *I*, settle down with
you and Magdalen ! Heaven help you !
I should be mad, or dead of it in a very

short time. It is a thousand pities you should think you have got anything to do with my concerns. Leave me alone, that's a good child. I'm past any mending of yours."

She still knelt by his chair, gazing, as if she would have forced the secret of his wild, unhappy nature to show itself. Perhaps she thought of the happy dark days she had read of, when holy women, by dint of fasting and prayer and faith, could master even such savage souls as Otho's—could cast forth devils, and so relieve the souls of wretched men. Those days must be past, for she could gather nothing from her searching gaze. Perhaps she was not holy enough. She had prayed, but she had not fasted ; and to judge from Effie's chatter, she had renounced none of the pomps and vanities of her station.

"You will be all right at the Dower House," Otho resumed presently. " Then you can have people to stay with you, and make yourself a little less dull. There! get up, don't look so desperately senti- mental. I am as I am; and I shall get along, if you'll leave me alone."

With that, he rose and put her aside, but gently and quietly; and she was almost sure that the hands which rested for a moment on her shoulders, quivered a little. .

Otho went into the smoking-room, shut the door, and turned up the light. He took a brandy decanter from a case of spirits which stood on the sideboard, and poured some into a glass; and this time there was no question as to his hand trembling. His lips, too, were unsteady. He drank the brandy, and muttered to himself—

"I must go and see Magdalen, or she will be suspicious. But not to-night— not to-night. Surely to-morrow will do. What was it she said to me that night about wronging her?"

He threw himself into a chair, and tried to collect his thoughts, and shape a coherent recollection of Magdalen's words. At last he had gradually pieced them together, and with them the scene in which they had been uttered—the great square, draughty vestibule before the Balder Hall door; the north-west storm wind screaming past it; his own figure, and that of Magdalen; the way in which they had stood close together, and the vows he had forced from her; and how at last she had put her hands upon his shoulders, and looked him straight in the eyes, and said that she did not claim any vows from him, but only bade him remember that whatever wrong he did her, directly or indirectly, from that day forth, he did to his wife, for that he was hers, as much as she was his.

" Well," he thought, as he laughed a feeble echo of his old blustering laugh, " it would not be the first time a man

had wronged his wife either ; but I
shan't. I shall tell the little baggage not
to make a fool of herself, but to keep
her languishing eyes for her bear of a
lover."

Otho, as he made these reflections, was
thinking of no one in London. His sister
had taken it for granted that he came
straight from his sojourn with Gilbert
Langstroth,—a very great mistake, as he
had driven that very morning from Friarsdale to Darlington, and taken the train
thence to Bradstane.

On the following day some kind of an
interview took place between Otho and
Magdalen. Eleanor saw very little of the
other. They were amicable when they
met, but nothing more. The day after
that Otho went into Friarsdale, not saying
that he was returning there, but simply
that he was going. Eleanor was thus
again left alone, and as soon as her young
visitor had returned to the vicarage, she

began her preparations for removing to
the Dower House.

One day, in the course of these preparations, she had cause to go into the shop of
Ada Dixon's father. Mrs. Dixon herself
came forward to serve her. She was, as
usual, stout, pompous, and important-look-
ing, had on a superfine gown, and a cap
which struck Miss Askam as being ridi-
culously young and small for her. Mrs.
Dixon wore it with an air, as if it had
been a coronet, which added to the absur-
dity of the spectacle. Eleanor had never
liked this woman, whose hard eyes and
want of simplicity and directness had
always offended her ; and she liked not
the air with which she now came forward.
But that it was (thought Eleanor) absurd
on the face of the thing, she would have
considered the glance bestowed upon her
by Mrs. Dixon as an insolent one. It
was at least hard, bold, and supercilious.
Not thinking it worth while to betray that

she had even noticed this manner, Eleanor
made her purchases, which were set aside
for her by Mrs. Dixon in lofty silence.
While she sought in her purse for the sum
with which to pay for the things, she inquired—

"How is your daughter, Mrs. Dixon?
I have not seen her lately."

"Thank you, Miss Dixon is very well."
(Eleanor repressed a smile on hearing
Ada's mother speak of her thus.)   "She
is not at home just at present.   She's
staying with some friends in Yorkshire
—in the Dales—some relations of Mr.
Dixon's."

"Oh yes?   In which of the Dales?"

"Wensleydale.   My husband's cousin
has a place there" (a large farm would
have been the correct description), "near
Bedale, it is."

"Oh, I hope she is enjoying herself."

"Oh, very much, thank you. She's
very much sought after— sixpence you will

want, I think—and they visit a good deal amongst the neighbours."

" Yes ?   And Mr. Camm ?   I hope you have good accounts of him ? "

" I really haven't heard anything about him lately," said Mrs. Dixon, in an indescribable tone, as she poised the fingers of both hands on the counter and looked out of the window, as if she thought the interview had better come to an end.

" Ah, I suppose Ada will be the person to get news of him.   I was so glad to hear he had done so well, and got such an excellent situation at Leeds.   Ada will like to live near a large town like that, I should think."

" Well, yes—perhaps.   Perhaps not," said Mrs. Dixon, with a glacial reserve, and then with crushing mysteriousness— " There's no saying where Ada may end, or what she's born to.   She is not a common girl, by any means."

" I hope she will end in marrying Mr.

Camm, and making him a very good wife. He is a first-rate young man, and deserves to be made happy," said Eleanor, nettled by the supercilious tone in which Roger's future mother-in-law spoke of him.

" Oh, he's a very worthy young man, I don't doubt," came the rejoinder; "a little rough, and wanting in polish—hardly the genteel manners one could desire."

" No, not very genteel, certainly," said Eleanor, hurrying a little in her desire to be able to laugh at leisure over the complaint that Roger Camm's manners were not " genteel." Indeed, they were not. If gentility were the desideratum, they were deplorably wanting, and likely to remain so.

Going up the street she suddenly met Michael Langstroth, and could not help telling him the joke, her eyes dancing as she spoke.

" Mr. Langstroth, do you know that for years you have cherished as your brother

a person—I can call him nothing else—
whose manners are· not genteel. At least,
Mrs. Dixon says they are not,—not as
genteel as she could wish in her son-in-
law—and she ought to know."

Michael looked at her searchingly for
a perceptible time, before he replied—

" At last you have heard something that
has made you laugh," said he. " I am
delighted, and Roger may congratulate
himself on his want of gentility, if it leads
even indirectly to that good result."

" Why—how—what do you know about
my laughing ? " she asked, crimsoning.

" Nothing, except that you don't do it
often enough. I wish I could give you
a prescription, but there is none for the
ailment that is want of mirth ; none in all
the pharmacopeia."

She took her leave of him, and walked
away. No, she thought ; the herb that
brings laughter is called heartsease, and
for her just now it grew not in Bradstane.

CHAPTER IV.

FIRST ALARM.

ONE day, very early in May, Michael Langstroth wrote from Bradstane to Roger Camm in Leeds :—

" A strong sense of duty alone induces me to trouble you with a letter, for there is literally no news to tell you. When was there ever any in Bradstane? And just now we are duller than usual, for nearly every one is away. People (the few who are left here) talk now off and on about the Derby, and speculate whether Crackpot will win. He is not the favourite, as of course you know, but takes a good place. I dare say I hear more of that

kind of thing than you do. The British
Medical people meet in Leeds this year.
Of course it won't be till August, but I
have every intention of going; and putting up with you; and I look forward
to it as if it were some wild dissipation.
It is, at any rate, too good a chance to be
missed of hearing and seeing something,
and getting one's blood stirred up generally. I often wonder I do not turn into
a mummy or a block of wood. On reading this you will probably leap to the rash
conclusion that your account of two political meetings, and their consequent excitement, has roused my envy and upset my
tranquillity, and that in future, you had
perhaps better not supply me with such
stimulating food! I beg you will not
cherish any such delusion. Your account
of the meetings was most interesting and
amusing; but as you know, I have a great
contempt for all political parties in the
abstract, and to see a vast body of men,

swayed like reeds by the passion of
the moment—groaning like demons when
they hear one set of names, cheering like
maniacs at another, falling like living
storm waves upon any unfortunate wight
who dares to express dissent from their
views, and hustling him out—is to me a
melancholy spectacle. You would doubt-
less say, that without such passions and
prejudices to be worked upon, things might
be at a standstill. I suppose they might:
all I know is, I am very thankful that there
are so many men in the world that my
indifference makes no difference. You
will wonder whence this sermon arises.
I have been meditating a good deal lately
o' nights; having felt tired when I came
in, and not having had your music to
govern my meditations, as in days of old.
And I was thinking, only last night, of
a dispute we used to have in our younger
days, about life and events. I always
maintained (quite wrongly, I confess now)

that you got no real *life*, no movement,
stimulus, animation, outside of a big city:
you vowed that, on the contrary, it is
the nature of the man that determines his
life, and that dramas and tragedies as full
of terror and pathos as Shakespeare's own,
might be played out within even as narrow
a compass as the township of Bradstane-
on-Tees, provided the actors were there,
and that they lived, not played their parts.
You were right, and I suppose you hold
the opinion still; but this is what I want
to know—how often is it that one gets
the chance to live? Most people would
answer, once at least, in a lifetime; and
there it is that I totally disagree with
them. Mine is a small stage from which
to preach, but I have seen as many people
as some who live on a larger one, and
I have observed them and their conditions
carefully. And, because of my profession,
the people I have seen have been of all
sorts and conditions, and the conclusion

I have come to is, that most lives are filled with emptiness—with a dead, dull uneventfulness. Action is for the favoured few; culture for a great many more, if they choose to avail themselves of it, which usually they don't; monotony for most.

" That brings me back to my own life, and its monotony. Let me try to collect a little gossip for you, and free myself from the reproach of having sent an essay, unredeemed by a single touch of narrative.

" Otho Askam is away. He has scarcely been at Thorsgarth since the new year. Just now he is busied, they say, about this precious horse which is to run this precious race. His sister's house, too, is empty just now. She was persuaded, Mrs. Johnson tells me, to go and see her friends in London for a time; but is coming back before Whitsuntide, as, in the kindness of her heart she is going to feast some little ragged wretches out of Bridge Street, whom she has taken

under her wing. But it is not Whitsuntide yet. It falls near the end of May
this year. I feel in a communicative
humour to-night, so I will tell you a secret.
My life is monotonous to me, as I believe
I have set forth already at some length;
and I wish with all my heart that Eleanor
Askam had not a fortune of twelve hundred a year; for if she had nothing at all,
I would humbly ask her if she would con-
descend to relieve that monotony of my
life. I should also have the feeling that
I could in a measure pay her back in kind,
by alleviating, as I would, some of the
sorrow that darkens hers.

"I believe I had something else to say
to you. I am almost certain that I sat
down with a distinct impression that I
was going to write to you about something. Oh yes, here it is. I suppose you
hear regularly from Miss Dixon, and so,
of course, you will know that a little while
ago, she returned from her long sojourn in

Wensleydale. I heard she had gone there for the pure air and all that, and because her father's relations wanted to have her, and because she did not feel very strong at the end of the winter. You know, I have always thought her a very delicate girl, but now—I do not think it right to conceal it from you—she looks very ill indeed. Her cheeks have fallen in ; her face is pale ; she is the shadow of what she was. I hate to write this ; in fact, I was so unwilling to write it, that I scribbled all the rubbish which premises it, in the hope that, somehow, I might get out of this ; but I cannot. It would be no friend's part; and what blame would you not have the right to put upon me, if I let it pass by without telling you. She is very ill, I am certain. If I were on different terms with them, I should go to Mrs. Dixon, and tell her she ought to have advice for her. I keep wishing they would summon me, or Rowntree ; for they surely must see themselves the change in her. I fancy she ought to go to a warmer climate, or rather, she ought never to have gone to Yorkshire. That part of Wensleydale where she was, is piercingly cold —worse than this. It is in a valley, but the valley itself is very much elevated. I do not want to make you more uneasy than is necessary. We must recollect that this is the 'merry month' of east winds, bronchitis, and pleurisy, and many a delicate girl withers up during May and comes out blooming again in June. Let us hope this is such a case. Sleep takes possession of me; therefore, good night!"

This letter had veritably been written in the way described in it. Michael had beheld Ada, and the change in her; and as Roger never, in any of his pretty frequent letters, mentioned any rumour of the illness of his betrothed, his friend reluctantly came to the conclusion that he knew nothing about it, and that to leave

him in such a state of ignorance was
utterly impossible for him. All the first
part of his letter he had written ramblingly, half his mind occupied with a
wonder whether he could not absolve himself from the moral necessity which he
felt upon him, of speaking about Ada. He
could not, and the result was the com-
position above, which was written on a
Wednesday night, and despatched on a
Thursday morning. Michael did not
expect any immediate answer to it, but
went about his business, as usual.

On the said Thursday morning, near
the Castle, he met Ada Dixon. There
was, indeed, a piercing east wind blowing,
and the girl wore a common-looking fur
cloak, with which her father had presented
her at Christmas, and of which she had
been proud, in that in shape and fashion
it bore a faint resemblance to the costly
garments in which Miss Wynter and Miss
Askam were in the habit of wrapping

themselves on cold days. Perhaps the dead black of the cloak showed up her pallor still more strongly by contrast; but as Michael met her—he was on foot, going to see a patient who lived beside the river-bank; she ascending a little hill, slowly and wearily, and he going down it—with her face a little upturned, and the flickering light quivering upon it through the leaves—her white hat and her fair hair,—as he met her thus, her appearance was almost spectral in its whiteness and fragility.

She inclined her head to him, and would have passed on. But he stopped, and held out his hand to her.

"Good morning, Miss Dixon. You must not think me meddlesome, but when Roger is not here, I consider you a little bit under my care; and my duty obliges me to tell you that you are not looking so robust as is desirable. Have you been catching cold?"

He was surprised at the effect of his words. Ada's white face became in a moment angrily red; the colour rushing over it in a flood. Her eyes flashed, and in a voice that was sharp with irritation, she said—

"Nothing ails me at all. I'm as well as I can be, and I think there's no call for you to make such remarks, Dr. Langstroth."

"I am sure I beg your pardon if I have offended you. I assure you there is nothing I less wish to do. I am very glad if you do feel well. Only, I wish you looked stronger—that is all."

"What do looks matter, when one feels perfectly well?" said Ada.

"There is certainly a good deal in that. Good morning. I will not detain you."

He raised his hat, and was moving on; indeed, he had walked a pace or two, when Ada's voice, just behind him, caused him to turn again. She looked embarrassed, and half-stammered, as she said—

" Oh, please—do you know—have you any idea when Miss Askam is coming home ? "

" I have not," said he gravely, and very much surprised. " At least, I know nothing of the exact day ; but before Whitsuntide, Mrs. Johnson says. She would know, I dare say, if you like to call and ask her."

" Oh, thank you ! I'll see. It's—it's not of so much importance," said Ada. " Good morning, Dr. Langstroth."

They parted. Michael went on his way, and as he went he shook his head.

" It is not of the least use for her to tell me that she is perfectly well. She is very ill indeed, and something ought to be done for her."

Many times during the day he thought of Ada, and of her changed looks, and

wondered how Mrs. Dixon would take it
if he spoke to her about her daughter.

About seven o'clock, just as he was
sitting down to his solitary dinner, his
dining-room door was opened, and Roger
Camm walked in.

Michael uttered an "ah!" of pleasure
and relief when he saw the mighty figure
lounge into the room.

"You here, Roger?" he said, jumping
up and grasping his hand. "Was it my
letter? Did you take the alarm?"

"Ay! I could not rest another day without coming to see that child. She scarcely
ever mentions her health; indeed, never;
so it never occurred to me that there could
be anything the matter with her."

"Then, my dear fellow, you must prepare
yourself for a very disagreeable surprise,
that's all. But have some dinner now,
and you can go down and see her afterwards."

Another place was set for Roger, who

made a praiseworthy effort to eat his
dinner, and to talk as if nothing had
happened. He could, however, scarcely
sit out the meal, and the instant it was
over he rose.

"I've come to you, feeling sure you
would put me up, Michael. I've got what
they call in Leeds 'the week-end,' and
must go off again by the late train from
Darlington on Sunday night."

"Of course you will put up here, and
I'll drive you into Darlington on Sunday.
I suppose you'll go out now?"

"Yes. Don't expect me back till you
see me," said Roger, going away; and
directly afterwards, Michael heard the door
shut after him.

CHAPTER V.

BROKEN OFF.

DESPITE that cutting east wind, it was a glorious May evening. The trees and fields were coming on grandly, and the sun shone dazzlingly towards his decline, in a heaven of bright blue and gold, with piles of glorified clouds in a steady bank to the north. The beams shone slantingly all on the old brown houses, and their rays were flashed back from the windows of the quaint old sleepy town. As Roger walked down the street, his heart beating with foreboding, he was but vaguely conscious of the stir of life around him, the murmur and bustle of those whose day's work was done, and who were enjoying their pipes, their gossip, and their games; for in one part of the town the youths played quoits in an open space, while many reverend elders looked on, and made sententious remarks as the sport progressed. He was conscious of receiving here and there a greeting; he returned them vaguely, and went on his way, and presently found himself within Mr. Dixon's shop, which looked very mean and low and small, and which seemed quite filled by his tall and broad figure. Mr. Dixon was alone in the shop.

"Bless my soul, Roger—you!" he exclaimed.

"Yes," replied Roger. "I got a couple of days' holiday, so I thought I'd run over and see Ada. Is she in?"

"Yes, she's in. You'll find her upstairs at her piano. The wife has gone out to tea. And look you, Roger," he added, drawing the young man aside, and lower-

ing his voice, though they were alone,
"Ada has got uncommon twiny and
washed-out-looking, and has taken to
singing the most sentimental songs. I
declare it makes me feel quite low in my
mind to hear her constantly wailing and
wailing. Try to cheer her up a bit."

"That I will!"

"I dare say she's just fretting a bit after
you."

Roger's heart bounded, and fell again.
It could not be so. Ada knew she needed
not to fret after him. But he said, as
cheerfully as he could—

"I'll go upstairs and find her."

With which he went through the shop
into the passage, and quickly up the stairs.
As he ascended, the "wailing" of which
Mr. Dixon had complained became distinctly audible. It was a very, very
mournful song that Ada sang, and Roger's
heart died within him as he heard it.

He opened the parlour door softly, and

looked in. The piano was opposite to the door; therefore Ada, seated at it, had her back turned towards him. She had ceased to play within the last minute, and sat very still, with her hands, he noticed, dropping down at her sides, in a way that had something very painful and hopeless about it. His heart went out to her, and as she did not at first appear to notice any sound or any footstep, he walked softly up behind her; but not so softly, big and heavy as he was, and unused to treading gingerly, but that she could hear him distinctly; and he noticed that she suddenly drew her hands up, and that they were clenched, and that her shoulders heaved, as if she drew a deep breath—not as if she were surprised, Roger thought, hope beginning to beat high in his heart again, *but rather as if she were very glad.* She knew, then, that he was there. She recognized his footstep, and she was moved, deeply moved, by his presence.

He laid his hands upon her shoulders, and said, softly and caressingly—

"Ada!"

She faced him, with the quickness of lightning, and with a veritable shriek,— it was too loud, too affrighted to be called an exclamation—and Roger recoiled before the expression of the face which was turned towards him.   He literally fell back a step or two, gazing at her alarmed and speechless, while she put her hands, one to either side of her head, and shrank together, staring at him with a look of terror and amaze.

"Ada, my love," he began at last, alarmed and bewildered by the contradiction between her manner before she had seen him, and that manner now that she beheld him.   Then she found her voice, and rose from the music stool.

"Roger, Roger!" she gasped.   "How can you! Stealing up behind one, and startling one in that way! It's enough

to turn the head, if one's a nervous person."

"But, my darling, I saw that you heard
me," he began; but she burst into hysterical
tears, turning away from him, and flinging
herself upon a sofa, so that he saw it was
useless to attempt to explain or apologize.
Once it crossed his mind, "She behaves
almost as if she had expected some one
else." Then he put the idea aside, as we
do put ideas aside which we know would
be absurd in regard to ourselves, often
without stopping to make allowances for
the differences in others' minds and our
own.

It was a very distressful scene. Nothing
that he could do or say restored calmness
to her, though the first violence of her
agitation presently wore off. In vain he
tried to wring from her some explanation
of her altered looks, her nervous terrors;
asked her what ailed her, and tenderly
upbraided her with not having told him

she was out of health. Ada would own
nothing, say nothing; and when he rather
pitifully said he had hoped to give her a
pleasant surprise by his unexpected arrival,
she replied with irritation that she hated
such surprises; he ought to have written
or telegraphed. In fact, Roger, with the
deepest alarm, presently saw that his
presence was doing her no good, but
harm; it was perfectly evident that he had
better retire, and he decided to do so.
But before going, he said—

"Now, look here, Ada. Grant me a
very great favour, and I'll not tease you
about anything else. Let Michael Langstroth, or Dr. Rowntree, see you. Rowntree, perhaps. He's such a kind, good old
fellow. He would give you something to
strengthen you."

"I am not ill," cried Ada; and she
stamped her foot on the ground, and
clenched her teeth. " I will see none of
your doctors. I hate them, and I'll have

nothing to do with them. You will *make* me ill, if you don't let me alone."

Every sign warned Roger that this was a subject it would be best not to pursue any further, and he presently left her. He had no heart to go into the shop again and speak to Mr. Dixon. Slowly and dispiritedly he made his way back to the Red Gables, and found Michael there, astonished to see him back again so soon, and looking the questions he felt he would not ask.

"I don't know, Michael," said Roger, in answer to this look. "There's something awfully wrong. I must see her father to-morrow. She denies that anything ails her, but at the same time she goes on in such a way as no one would who was all right. It is not the end—I know it is not the end."

On the following day it seemed as if the end, so far as Roger was concerned, had arrived. In the forenoon Mr. Dixon

made his appearance, and asked to see
Roger. Then, slowly and with difficulty,
he unfolded the fact that Ada had summoned him to her after her lover's departure, and had told him that she could
never be Roger's wife; that her life was
a misery to her, so long as she was
engaged to him, and that if her father
wished to see her well and happy again,
he was to take this opportunity of telling
Roger so, and of making him understand
that she did not wish to see him again.

The stout, prosperous tradesman looked
pinched and miserable as he told his
sorry tale; while the young man sat opposite to him, his face turning very white,
his strong hands shaking, and his mighty
figure trembling all over, like a leaf in the
wind. The sun was shining outside,
though not into the room; one could see
its glare in the yellow hue of the grass, and
the shadows cast by the trees. The sound
of singing birds came in at the open

window, and also a blast of north-east
wind, cold, dry, cutting as a knife.

"She does not mean it, Mr. Dixon; she
does not really mean it?" he stammered,
fighting for his life.

"She means it, Roger. I wrestled with
her about it for an hour; for with expecting you to be my son for so long, I've got
to look upon you as if you were my son.
I wrestled with her till I saw she was
nigh to fainting, and then I had to stop.
She pulled this off her finger, and told me
to give it you."

He pulled a little pearl ring from his
pocket, and pushed it across the table
towards Roger, without looking at him,
Roger picked it up, and turned it round in
his fingers as if he did not know what it
was—as if the sight of the little jewels
dazed him.

"She said she wished to send no unkind
words, for that perhaps she'd never see
you again; but that you must not come

nigh her, for another scene with you would kill her, and she wants to live."

"Let her live then," said Roger, in a hoarse and laboured voice. "It does not matter what becomes of me."

Mr. Dixon, sturdy philistine that he was, wiped his eyes with his handkerchief.

"Roger," he said, with a solemnity and strength of conviction which gave dignity and something like majesty to his commonplace, outside man, "you have just cause to look upon my girl with suspicion, and to fight shy and speak ill of us all. But, lad, I tell you, we don't know the end of it all yet. I can tell you, my heart is heavy. There's a weight on it, as if something uncommon was coming, or hanging about in the air somewhere. I can't mind my business, nor eat my victuals, for thinking of that girl, that looks like a ghost; and why, that's what I want to know—why?"

"I'm afraid," said Roger, in a laboured
voice, but instinctively trying to give comfort to the man who was older and weaker
than himself, "that she may have begun
to care for some one else, who perhaps
doesn't respond as she could wish.   If so,
it is best for her to be free from me."

"Choose what it is, it's a heavy trouble
for us all," said Mr. Dixon wearily.   "I'm
often afraid that she was brought up with
notions far above her station,—Miss Wynter, and all that ; but somehow, I never
took it to be anything seriously wrong. . . .
You'll not look upon me as an enemy,
Roger, for I've fought for you through
thick and thin ? "

"An enemy—God forbid !   I know you
have been my friend all through."

"We are going to send her away," pursued Mr. Dixon.   "She has asked to go
down to my sister in Devonshire, a widow,
who has often wanted to have a visit from
her.   She says, if she gets away from all

this ("all what?" thought Roger, a thick
dread at his heart—" her home, her friends,
her natural life, with all its hopes and
interests?"), once away, she thinks she'll
be better. So we shall send her. I won't
stay. I've dragged myself here, and I
shall drag myself back again. Can you
shake hands with me, my lad?"

Roger unhesitatingly gave him his hand,
went with him to the door, and saw him
walk away; then returned, to try and
understand the meaning of what had be]
fallen him. He was surprised to find that
after a time, instead of reproaching Ada,
even in thought, he was occupied in trying
to recall any occasions on which he might
have spoken harshly to her, and in mentally
imploring her to forgive him his trespasses,
and in wishing that he had but the chance
to do it in so many words; while his sense
of the mysterious terror that hung over
her grew greater every moment. He did
not leave Bradstane earlier than he had

intended. A great calm and a great pity
had settled upon his soul. He found himself able to speak freely to Michael of
what had happened—to tell him more of
his inner thoughts and feelings than, in all
their long intimacy, he had ever divulged
before. He told Michael what Ada was
going to do, and he said—

"When she comes back, for my sake,
Michael, you will pay a little heed to her,
and let me know how she looks, at any
rate."

"You may trust me to do it."

"It is all quite over between us. I have
a feeling that that is quite certain ; but I
don't feel as if we knew everything yet.
And God forbid that I should judge her
in the dark. A girl doesn't carry on as
she is doing, either from lightness of mind
or hardness of heart."

This was as Michael drove him along
the lanes to Darlington to catch the night
train. Michael said nothing. Friendship

demanded that what Roger required of him in this matter, he should do, whatever he might think of the cause of his friend's distress.

CHAPTER VI.

HOW CRACKPOT WAS SCRATCHED.

THEY left the dogcart outside the station, and Michael went in with Roger to see him off. As he stood beside the carriage window, waiting for the train to start, Roger, leaning out of the window, said to him in a low voice—

" I haven't forgotten what you said to me, Michael, though it looks as if I had—what you said in your letter about a certain lady."

" I did not suppose you had forgotten," replied Michael, gravely and simply; " but I think you had better do so. Consider that I wrote it in a fit of momentary weakness of mind. Indeed, if I could have borne to write the last part of the letter over again, I would not have sent the first, when it came to the point."

"It is safe enough with me ; but I can't quite see why you should call it weakness. Look here, Michael, we both know how that lady is situated, and you say you wish she had not got twelve hundred a year of her own. Take my word for it, if she knew that, she would curse her money. Don't go to suppose that I have not eyes in my head, and ears to hear with."

They had clasped hands, and the train had begun very slowly to move. Roger went on rapidly—

"I hoped at first that you never would care for her, when I began to see that she attracted you. Now I believe she is the woman to make you happy, as you are the man to do the same thing by her. Go in, and win, Michael, and never heed what the black things about her may say. Good-bye, old friend, and luck go with you."

There was a hard pressure of the two hands, which then had to be unclasped. The train glided out. Michael was left upon the platform, looking after it. When it had disappeared, he went outside again, found his dogcart, gave a coin to the boy who had held the horse—for he had brought no servant, wishing to have Roger to himself on the drive ; and now he set off on his return journey.

When he drove out of Darlington it was after eleven o'clock ; there was a radiant full moon hanging in the sky, and the whole land was flooded with its beauty and its brilliance. The roads, after he had got out of the town, were solitary and silent, as country roads, late on a Sunday night, are wont to be. He had all the beauty, all the glamour of the night to himself, and it sank into his soul, and the words which Roger had uttered resounded in his mind, like a refrain. He did not drive very fast. He was in no

mood to tear along, but was rather disposed to taste to the full the cup of
beauty and graciousness that was offered
to him. One by one, he drove through
the chain of exquisite villages which make
that road one of the most beautiful in all
England,—Coniscliffe, Piercebridge, Gain-
ford, and Winston, arrived at which place,
for the sheer pleasure of the further drive,
and the enjoyment of the pure night air,
and the magic of the scene and the hour,
he turned off, instead of pursuing his way
straight, to one side, and took the round-
about and surpassingly beautiful road
which leads through Ovington, and past
Wycliffe Hall and wood, and its ancient
little church of solemn beauty, and so
across Whorlton Bridge to Bradstane.
Every inch of the way was beautiful.
And that which lent the greatest charm
to it was the river, which, ever as he
drove, he had near him. Now he lost
it ; again it gleamed suddenly on his sight,

emerging unexpectedly into the open, from
some deep wood, or rushing in a sweeping curve into view ; now sunk between
marly banks, now making its way "o'er
solid sheets of marble grey." Grand old
Tees! thought Michael, paying it a paren-
thetical tribute, in the midst of the many
other thoughts which just then crowded
his mind, and made the long drive seem
to him a short one; where was it to be
matched for beauty and stateliness, and
natural grandeur, and wild, unbounded
variety ? How different here, as it flowed
on steady and strong, from what it was
as it came, little more than a fierce, brawling mountain stream, tearing over the wild
moors near its source! It had been his
friend and companion through many a
weary year, as he had gone his rounds,
wide and long as the valley itself. Like
all such friends, ungifted with the deceit-
ful power of human language, it had
always had the very voice that suited his

mood. In his youth, no longings had been too high, and no hopes too feverish for it to encourage. And for ten years, since he had been a veritable man, it had been his constant guide and associate. In spring it rushed joyfully along, singing a song of encouragement ; in summer its cool surface and the soothing murmur of its flow had many a time made tolerable the burden and heat of the day. He had heard its autumn roar, and in wilder moods had ridden races with it ; and he knew its aspect in winter, gray and sullen, or even iron-bound almost all its length, from mouth to source ; in its smoother expanses covered with skaters, or laden with blocks of ice, which, when the thaw wind began to blow, split and parted with reports like explosions, and then went sailing in beautiful glistening blocks towards the sea.

Just now, in this May moonlight, at the hour which was neither night nor

day—for midnight was past—it fulfilled
its spring vocation ; and as he drove along,
its murmur swelled out into the night,
and held out promises—promises so brave
and high that he mistrusted them almost.
And yet, a voice in his heart told him,
with an unerring whisper, that he might
believe these promises ; that if he went
and asked Eleanor Askam to confirm their
truth, she would do so. The knowledge
thrilled him ; it was pungent—half-bitter,
half-sweet. It gave him a new sense of
youth, a conquering confidence to which
he had long been a stranger. He rejoiced in it, and rejoiced greatly all the
while that he shook his head, and said
within himself " impossible," and repeated
that he wished she were not so rich—so
much richer than he was. If anything
should happen—some transitory misfortune, by which she might for one moment
feel herself quite poor, and believe she
had no resting-place for her head, and

he the next moment might bid that dear
head rest where it should ever be welcome—on his own heart—ah, Bradstane
town and the cobble-stoned streets, the
Red Gables and reality !

On the following day he heard that Ada
Dixon had gone to stay with her father's
widowed sister, at some remote Devonshire
village. The sister had been housekeeper
to a great family in the neighbourhood ;
had married the butler, and was now living
partly on the fruits of her own savings,
partly on a pension from the said family.

"Poor Roger !" reflected Michael. "If
the girl were something very wonderful, or
very gifted, or marvellously attractive, one
could forgive such connections. And there's
no harm in poor old Dixon ; but as for the
others—no, they are not suited for him."

The little bit of gossip and talk caused
by this second visit of Ada Dixon to
friends at a distance, following so rapidly
upon her return from a first absence, had

had time to die away, and the middle of
May had arrived, when Michael became
aware that his new neighbour, Miss Askam,
had returned from her sojourn amongst her
friends. The Dower House showed signs
of life; the windows were filled with pots
of flowering plants, and one or other of the
little Johnsons began to be frequently seen
on the doorsteps, while the Thorsgarth
landau came round every fine afternoon,
and was driven into the country with Miss
Askam and one or more either of these
little Johnsons, or their hard-worked
mamma, or Mrs. Parker; for the young
lady seemed to have no pleasure in solitary
state drives. Sometimes, on his rounds,
Michael met her, and then there was a
bow on his part, and a secret thrill of
delight, and perhaps some of the power
he felt showing in his eyes; and a gracious
inclination, an irrepressible brightness
overspreading her face, on her side. A
week or ten days passed, by no means

ungenially, in this way, till the Derby week arrived.

On the Monday morning Michael was amazed to receive a note from Eleanor.

" MY DEAR MR. LANGSTROTH,

" I wonder if you would think it very troublesome to come and tell me, if by any chance you *should* hear anything about my brother's horse, on Wednesday. I am most anxious to know, and thought perhaps you might know people who will have telegrams about the race before Thursday's paper comes. I shall not see that till the afternoon, you know.

" Sincerely yours,

" E. ASKAM."

Michael, as she conjectured, had means of gaining information before Thursday's London paper made its appearance. He wrote to the secretary of a certain club at

Darlington, desiring him to telegraph to him any news of " Crackpot," at as early a date as possible. He was both astonished and disturbed to receive a telegram on the Tuesday night, and its contents were not too soothing to his feelings. Thinking it best to get the business over at once, he went straight to the Dower House, and was admitted to Miss Askam at once.

She looked astonished to see him, and he perceived that her brightness was gone. There was a look of worn and harassed anxiety, and of nervous restlessness, too, about her. Her hands trembled, and her eyes wavered.

" Miss Askam," he was beginning, but she interrupted him.

" You have got a telegram. Something has happened. I knew it. I had—I was certain of it. What is it,—because I know the race is not yet run ? Is anything the matter with Otho ? "

" This telegram," he began again.

" Please let me read it.   I cannot wait."

He handed it to her silently, and it fluttered in her hands as she perused it ;—

" *Crackpot scratched.   No end of a row.*"

" I do not know what that means," she said tremulously.   " Scratched—will you please explain."

" It means," said he reluctantly, "that your brother has withdrawn his horse· at the last moment from the race ; and from the last part of the telegram, I am afraid there must be an impression that — that—— "

" That he has not dealt honourably," she said, quickly and breathlessly.   " I want to know a little more, please, Mr. Langstroth. Is it not usual to withdraw a horse in this way ? "

" No.   At least, it is a great pity when it has to be done.   It is particularly a great pity that your brother should have had to do it the first time a horse of his was running. Some men do it pretty often; and then, you know, they get a bad name, and are not considered——"

"Honourable. I understand. But will he have done it without any reason? Can you say, just at the last, 'I have changed my mind, and my horse shall not run?'"

"Most likely it is given out that Crackpot is ill, and unfit to run. Nay, it may be that he is so. Do not distress yourself about it," he added eagerly. "I will find out all that I can about it, and let you know. Everything will be uncertain now, of course."

She was still standing by the table, looking at him with haggard eyes, and as he spoke thus, she shook her head.

"No, no!" said she. "Just once, while I was in London, I happened to be at a regatta, with my friends, and Otho was there, too. And I saw a disagreeable-looking man come up to him, who did not know I had anything to do with him.

They talked together for a little while, and
I did not hear what they said, till suddenly
the man said, ' But mind you, Askam, none
of your tricks.   You are a slippery cus-
tomer at the best.'   I felt so indignant
that I turned round quite angrily ; and then
he saw that I knew Otho, and they laughed,
and moved a little to one side."

" I don't see that that incident has any
necessary connection with this," said he
quietly.   " You can do nothing, you know,
Miss Askam.   Do not distress yourself
needlessly.   To do that is to render yourself powerless when any real emergency
arises."   •

" Yes, I know," said she, and paused.
He looked at her, and saw that she looked
worn and anxious.

" Is there anything else I could do for
you ? " he began.   " Because I should be
so glad——— "

" No,   thank   you,   nothing,   except   to
promise   that   should   you   hear   anything

more about the thing, you will let me know."

" That I certainly will," said he, and rose to take his leave. " You still remain amongst us, in Bradstane," he observed gravely, but kindly, as he held out his hand.

" Yes," said Eleanor, with a quick flush. " I do not wish to go away. I—I intend to stay here."

" Always ? "

" I think—always."   She spoke steadily, but did not look at him.

" I am very glad to hear that," replied Michael quietly. " Now I know you are strong when you choose to be so. Will you promise not to fret foolishly over the thing—not to brood and mope over it ; or else I shall be sorry I complied with your request ? "

" I promise to behave as well as in me lies," said Eleanor, smiling.

" Then, good evening."

He went away thoughtful.   He knew
perfectly well that she would have to hear
more disagreeable things about Otho before very long, but he had succeeded in
lulling her fears for the present, at any
rate.

CHAPTER VII.

" CARELESSE CONTENTE."

THE withdrawal of Crackpot from the running, on the very day before the race, made a great sensation in the world of the turf. The affair was looked upon with suspicion, especially in connection with Otho Askam's known character for slipperiness—a character which stuck to him, although no one could exactly say how he had first got it. But the sensation was very much confined to the circles immediately connected with the event. Otho had managed with sufficient skill to avoid having anything tangible brought up against him. The rumours that were

current did not penetrate to his sister's
ears. The things that were written about
the circumstance were published in sporting or "society" papers, which she never
saw, and in their own peculiar jargon.
Michael, in his rounds, heard it all freely
discussed, but was careful never to let her
know what he heard. He wished her to
forget it, and presently it seemed as if she
did. At her age, and with her tempera-
ment, the heart, though it is peculiarly
sensible to sorrow, and feels it with a
keenness resembling resentment, is also
very open to joy; and there were joyful
influences at work in her life that summer.
Michael did not even tell her of the
rumours he had heard, that Otho had lost
a great deal of money by withdrawing
Crackpot from the race; for after all, they
were rumours, and not substantiated facts,
though Michael believed them to be true
enough. Otho had what Michael considered the good taste not to come near

Thorsgarth after his escapade, and for a season the land had rest from him and his presence.

It has been said that there were joyful influences at work in the life of Eleanor this summer; and that was true. Her nature loved sunshine, and just now it had it in plenty, both moral and material. From May—after the bad news about Otho—till August, sunlight prevailed. There was a long, hot, glorious summer, such as is not often vouchsafed to us nowadays. Hitherto she had known Bradstane literally only under its winter aspect. These months offered a variety of view and climate; and she, keenly and intensely sensitive to such influences, rejoiced with the rejoicing summer. Her life at the Dower House just then was a far from unpleasant one. She had gathered round her a little circle of friends, both young and old, and they gave freshness and variety to her life, as she helped to bring charm and poetry into theirs. She began for the first time really to understand what pleasure money can give—the possession of it, that is, and the power which that possession confers of affording pleasure and relief to others. She helped to make the summer golden to others beside herself. Amongst the pleasures of that season, there were none she enjoyed more than the out-of-door life which the unusual fineness and dryness of the summer rendered possible. There were day-long excursions, begun early in the morning, and only ended when the dew and the night were falling together—excursions into the deep woods, over the glorious moors, or beside the lovely streams which water and adorn that wild and beautiful tract of Borderland, called Teesdale. Sometimes she and her friends, the little Johnsons, would set off alone, swarming (the children) in and out of a pony chaise which never seemed too small, however many got into it; and which was yet never too large, even when there were not more than two or three to occupy it. As often as not the old doctor would be their guide and chaperon; and under his direction they explored the country for miles around. It was new to Eleanor; it was mostly new to her young companions, who had never before had a fairy with a pony chaise to take them about. This was very pleasant, with the lunches eaten "by shallow rivers," or under leafy trees; when the children splashed and waded to their heart's content, and the days, long though they were, never seemed long enough.

But there were also other and larger affairs, more important in every sense of the word,—proper picnics, at which several parties joined,—the Johnsons, Dr. Rowntree and his sister, Mrs. Parker, Eleanor; and on one or two occasions, even Michael had managed to snatch a day and join them, leaving his work to his assistant. On one of these days when he was present, they explored Deepdale ; on another they managed to climb " Catcastle Crag." On both of these occasions it was noticed that Michael's behaviour was marked by an unaccountable levity, and Miss Askam's by a kind of laughing apprehension. She, too, seemed to see jokes where no one else could detect them. Michael, indeed, went so far as to tell the children that this was not the first time that Miss Askam had been to Catcastle, and having by means of sundry mysterious hints roused their curiosity to fever pitch, and set them to attack her with every kind of question they could think of, he fell into the rear, and conversed with Mrs. Parker, leaving Eleanor to baffle them as best she could.

They happened to be alone for a few moments on the occasion of the Deepdale expedition, and he seized the opportunity to say—

" I notice that you still retain that in-

genuous youth, William, for your special
body-servant ; I suppose it is his complete
incapacity which recommends him to you ?
You do not like to dismiss him, because
you are quite sure no one else would take
him on ; and you think it is better that he
should have the semblance of an occupation than that you should have to support
him by charity."

"You wrong poor William, Mr. Langstroth. He is a very good servant, and
a most faithful creature." ·

"So I should fancy. He knows the
country almost as well as his mistress
does, and has such wonderful presence
of mind, as to make him invaluable in any
emergency."

"Well, I think he has the presence of
mind, at any rate, to know when help
was nigh."

"Say, rather, the power of lung to in-
voke that help when it was afar off. You
don't know what a long way I rode

back, summoned by that unearthly yell of his."

Eleanor laughed. "Poor William!" she said.

"Ah, I do admire William. Do you see, he knows we are talking about him, and the children are beginning to be suspicious too. I believe William fears we are going to ask him to act as guide to some place. Would you mind my catechizing him a little on the geography of the district? It would keep him up to the mark, you know, and would be such a useful thing for the children as well."

"Please don't, Mr. Langstroth. You will make me look ridiculous before them all."

"If I have seen you looking ridiculous, and if William has seen you looking ridiculous," said Michael, "as we certainly did, you know, on a never-to-be-forgotten occasion, what can it matter if a set of children and their mother see the same thing?"

"Oh, nothing, perhaps," was the sweet reply. "But are you sure you did not look a little ridiculous too? And if Effie once had her confidence in your infallibility shaken—— "

"That is true. Like the villains in novels, you have a power over me, through the innocent ones whom I love. I will keep silence this time, but take care how you provoke me too far."

"Do not be so childish."

This was very frivolous nonsense, and they enjoyed it, as they enjoyed the hot summer sun, the cool streams, the shady woods, and even the fun they had in combating the swarms of wasps which usually followed them in these expeditions, and entirely frustrated their efforts to sit down, and, as Effie plaintively said, "eat a meal in peace."

Once, deeper feelings were touched, and this was on a day when they had penetrated further than ever before; and on

this occasion, too, Michael was with them.
Setting off very early, they drove in the
morning coolness to Middleton-in-Tees-
dale, and thence onwards to High Force,
where they rested and lunched ; after which
they drove onwards to some little huts
at the edge of the moor, where path
ended, and wilderness began ; when they
got out, and walked for a mile and a
half to the wild spot where Tees comes
first winding, sluggish and sinuous, over
the moor top, in what is called the Weel,
and then suddenly precipitates himself
madly over " Caldron Snout," tearing down
an incline of two hundred feet to the lower
level, where he pursues a brawling way
towards High Force, his next descent.

This is a very wild and desolate spot,
and requires intrepid walking to get to it ;
plunging through the thymy moor, rough,
pathless, and uneven, without guide, save
for rough wooden posts like crosses,
planted at intervals of several hundred

yards, to show the directest way to the cataract. But so few persons visit Caldron Snout, so few tourists or picnicers care to be at the trouble of penetrating to it, that no road has got beaten out. Nature seems to sit enthroned in undesecrated queenliness in the fastnesses around the cataract.

It was a day that Michael and Eleanor never forgot. The children, literally frantic with the novelty and the wildness of the thing, and with the exhilarating moorland air, tore about in all directions—over heather and thyme, bluebells and boulders. Now came a scream of joy, and a mad rush to Michael or the doctor to ask the name of some hitherto unknown plant or flower —as the delicate autumn gentian, or, on some grassy banks, the poetical looking fragile " grass of Parnassus." Anon, wonder, quite awed and hushed, and treading on tiptoe to peep into a nest concealed beneath the grass, and containing five dirty-white eggs, with wine-coloured splashes on them. Then on again, to fresh fields and pastures new, till one wild whoop announced the discovery, in its steep hidden gorge, of the waterfall itself.

The elders walked more sedately, rejoicing with joy more cultivated, if not more intense, in the larger grandness of great, sweeping lonely fells, of miles of purple heather ; and in the abstract impressiveness of such a solitary torrent as Caldron Snout.

It was as they were wending back towards their vehicles, in the evening, that Michael and Eleanor found themselves alone. The children were scattered, making the most of what time remained to them, for the collection of interesting natural objects. Mrs. Johnson, with an eye to her rockery at home, had stopped in front of a patch of fine bog-plants, and had made the doctor go on his knees, armed with an old table knife. She was standing over him, directing him to the finest plunder, perfectly deaf to his assurances that the fine purple pinguicula which she coveted could find lovely flies here for its sustenance, but that its poor carnivorous leaves would most likely shrivel up and die in the dark corner of her garden, devoted to the cultivation of ferns and houseleeks.

At some distance from these two Michael and Eleanor stood side by side, facing Mickle Fell, and gazing at the noble sight unfolded for their delight. Many a time Eleanor had seen this grand old mountain in the distance, overtopping his comrades, always; but now he rose straight before them, apparently not a mile away. They were both struck by what they saw. The great fell, who seemed to spring aloft from the smaller ones which clustered about him, formed a centre and a focus to the picture, rising in a blunt, massive kind of point. His huge and grim sides were clothed in

a violet veil of summer haze and heat, like
a garment such as no earthly hands ever
fashioned.   This was beautiful; but it was
not all.   The sun stood, at the moment
when it seemed to rest exactly on the mid-
most point of his summit, a blazing golden
ball, and rays streamed away from it on
every side, so that Mickle Fell seemed
veritably to wear a crown of glory, sur-
passing all the crowns and all the jewels
of all the kings in the whole world.   Just
at the moment, the stillness was utterly
unbroken.   Not even the murmur of the
torrent reached them, nor the voices of
the children " playing in the light of the
setting sun."   Earth seemed to hold her
breath while one of her great hills received
the crown and the benediction of the
closing day.   No hum of booming bee,
no voice even of any bird, broke the dead
silence; nor did these two venture to dis-
turb it, but gazed and worshipped, and felt
that even if they lived to be very old, they

would not often see the heavens declare
the glory of God so sublimely as at this
moment.

And it was but for a moment; such
scenes seldom last longer. Suddenly
things seemed to change; the glory became
dimmed; sounds became audible; the
spell was loosed; and with one deep sigh
both their hearts confessed it, as their
eyes met.

Perhaps they both understood at that
moment, though all that Michael said, was,
"I am very glad that we have seen that—
together."

"So am I," she rejoined softly.

Then suddenly, almost at their feet,
broke forth a gossipy, importunate, "Brek-
kek-kek!" and behind them children's
voices shouted. They smiled. The awe
and the solemnity had gone, but the joy
remained and was abiding. It did not die
away, even after the sun had set and the
golden rays were quenched in night. It

made itself felt all through the long drive home through the darkling lanes, and it breathed out of the delicious scent of the firwoods, beneath which part of their road lay. It looked out of the eyes of both, as they clasped hands and parted after it was all over.

That was the last of some cloudlessly happy days. It was, in reality, the first day of Michael's summer holiday, and he knew it would be the best. On the following morning he set off to Leeds, where that year the British Medical Association had its annual meeting; after which, he and Roger were going to take a short country tour together.

One evening, in August, soon after Michael had gone, Eleanor was startled to see Otho walk into her drawing-room, looking ill and haggard. He threw himself into a chair, gave a long kind of sigh, and asked her how she did.

CHAPTER VIII.

THE SHADOW.

IT seemed as if, when Otho came in, joy went out. Eleanor, as she viewed his sinister figure, and saw his haggard countenance, felt a chill steal over her in the midst of the August warmth. It was like the first breath of winter, sent as a warning when autumn days are mild and life delicious.

"You have come back at last, Otho. Are you going to stay at Thorsgarth?"

"Just for two or three days. I've been there and put up my traps, and I meant to stay there, but it is such a dismal hole. It makes me creep all over. I could not stand it, so I thought I would look in upon you."

"I am glad you did," she said, wondering a little why he had chosen rather to visit her than Magdalen. But she did not ask, and he did not mention the subject. He did not stay very long. She asked him if he came from London, and he said yes. She did not ask him about Gilbert. She had nearly forgotten him. The strength of the love she felt for Michael had effaced almost the recollection of the uncomfortable days she had passed during Gilbert's Christmas visit, and the fears she had felt with regard to him.

"I thought you would be coming before," she said, "for the shooting. People are saying it is something unheard of for you to be without a party at Thorsgarth just now."

"People may mind their own business. It doesn't suit me to have a party. I can't afford."

"Are you poor, Otho? Have you been losing money?"

"What a question to ask! If you inquired whether I'd got any money left *to* lose, it would be more to the point."

"I am very sorry to hear it. Are you going already?" For he had risen.

"Yes, I arranged with a fellow to meet me at home at eight, and it's nearly that now."

"I shall see you to-morrow?"

"I shall be busy in the day, but at night—yes, I'll come and dine with you, Eleanor. What time?"

"Seven, Otho; but come as soon as you like, and I'll invite Magdalen to spend the evening too."

"Magdalen!" He looked startled, as he had done on a former occasion, and not too well pleased. Then he said, with an attempt at indifference—

"Oh, all right. That will be the best way."

He departed, and as it was not too late, Eleanor sent a note by that night's post, telling Miss Wynter that Otho was over, and would dine with her the following evening. Would she (Magdalen) join them and spend the evening?

Magdalen sent a man the next day with her acceptance of the invitation, and Eleanor awaited her two guests with the feelings of one who is heroically going through a most disagreeable duty.

It was the end of August, and on quiet, cloudy days it was twilight by seven o'clock. Just before that hour Eleanor had occasion to go into one of the front rooms;—her dining and drawing-rooms were at the back, looking upon a pleasant garden and orchard, and the front rooms were small ones, separated from these others by folding doors.

She got what she wanted, and then paused for a moment beside the window, looking out upon the street, which was

grey with the dusk, and the houses over
the way did not show very clearly. No
one was about except, as Eleanor noticed,
a woman, whom she had seen earlier in the
afternoon, in another part of the town ; an
itinerant singer, who had been going from
door to door, singing ballads and collect-
ing money. Eleanor had noticed her, and
had been struck with the decency of her
appearance, and the unusual quietness and
modesty of her look. She had told her
servants, if the young woman came to her
house, to take her into the kitchen, and
give her a meal. This had been done,
and the girl now seemed not to intend to
sing any more. She had been going about
bareheaded ; now she had put on a small
straw bonnet, and placed a woollen shawl
about her shoulders. She stood near the
doorsteps, and looked this way and that, as
if not certain in which direction to go.
The window was open, and Eleanor was
about to throw it still higher up, and sug-

gest to the young woman where she might find a lodging for the night, when quick steps approached from that side of her own house at which she stood. Then a man's figure, in a light summer overcoat and a round hat, appeared; it was Otho, and he had one foot on the doorstep, when the young woman turned, and began rather timidly—

" If you please, sir—— "

" Good God! what do you mean!" he exclaimed in a voice in which both fear and anger struggled. " Have you no more—— "

"Sir!" exclaimed the young woman, facing him fully, and in evident astonishment, " I was not going to beg—I—— "

" Confound you!" burst from Otho's lips, and his voice trembled, with what emotion Eleanor could not guess. " You made me think—what do you want, loafing about here ? "

" I am doing no such thing as loafing,"

said the young woman in high dudgeon.
" I am a respectable woman, and I was
going to ask you a civil question—that's
all. But I'll go further on, now."

She turned away, indignation quivering
in her every movement. Otho stood still
a moment, Eleanor noticed, as she breathlessly watched and listened, with his hand
resting against the door pillar, as if to
support himself. And she saw that he
pulled out his handkerchief and wiped his
brow; and she heard something muttered
between his teeth, and then the words,
" cursed hole like this ! " Then he came
into the house, for the door opened from
the outside, and she mechanically went
out to meet him, disturbed more than she
would have cared to own. For whom,
for what had he mistaken the young
woman, that he should show such alarm
and such fear ?

He was standing in the hall, having laid
his hat upon the table, and was pulling off

his overcoat. His face was quite white,
or rather, gray, and his eyes looked wild
and startled.

"Halloa!" said he, evidently with an
effort—at least, it was evident to her now
that she knew what had gone before.
"How are you? Has Magdalen come?"

"No. I am expecting her every
minute," she replied. "Ah, there are the
carriage wheels. She is here now."

Otho was now master of himself again.
He waited in the hall till Magdalen had
come in, and received her, looking into her
eyes with a sort of eagerness, and kissing
her as he looked at her.

The evening proved, in a way, less
depressing than Eleanor had expected.
Magdalen was unusually sweet and
gracious; Otho more genial and expan-
sive than his sister had ever seen him.
Magdalen openly and unreservedly put
questions to him about his affairs and
intentions, which Eleanor would never

have dreamed of asking. He was not very explicit as to his business, but said it was business that brought him to Thorsgarth, adding with candour that nothing else would induce him to set foot in the place, for he had got a horror of it. From some hints that he let fall, the two young women gathered that his stables and stud were to come to the hammer—when, he did not say. Also, that he was at present somewhat straitened for any considerable sum of money. But he did not hint at any wish to borrow money, or receive assistance, only saying that Gilbert would see him safe through present difficulties, and that the Friarsdale stables would bring in " a pot of money."

" I'm going to Friarsdale to-morrow," he added, " and back here the same night. The day after, I'm off again."

" Are you ? Where ? "

" London first. Then Paris, I expect. I've got some business there," he con-

descended to inform them, " in connection
with the *Grand Prix* next spring.

" Racing again ! " said Magdalen. " But
you've got no horse in it."

" Yes, but I have. I've Crackpot again."

" *Again !* " repeated Miss Wynter, with
emphasis and meaning.

" Oh, it's all straight this time. You
need not be sneering, Mag ; and Eleanor
need not turn up her eyes in that lacka-
daisical fashion. When Crackpot has won
the *Grand Prix*, as I intend him to, I shall
sell him for—well, a good lot of money.
Then I shall be fairly on my legs again.
Thorsgarth may stay as it is, yet awhîle,
and the timber can remain in the woods."

" I should hope so ! " exclaimed Eleanor,
in a voice of alarm.

" And if you'd only marry me now,
Magdalen, out of hand, you should have
the purse-strings, and keep me in order.
Come, let it be a bargain ! "

Magdalen's eyes glittered. It was a

bargain she would have clinched that moment if she could.

"You know it is utterly impossible, Otho, now. But if you'll come home again before Christmas — well before Christmas, you know, I might be able to settle things."

"Oh, do promise, Otho !" Eleanor urged him eagerly. "If only you and Magdalen could get married at the end of this year or the beginning of next—why, you might go abroad ; and when you had got this money that you speak of, you might live abroad."

Her heart leaped up at the idea that Magdalen, if she once had him in hand, and was as he said mistress of the purse-strings, might have a strong influence over him, and that, having broken from his sporting associates, both here and in London, something different—something a little better, might surely be made of him.

"If you would marry him, Magdalen,"

she went on, " I would spend the rest of
the winter myself with Miss Strangforth,
if she would have me ; or you could find
her another niece to come and live with
her."

" I would do my best," Magdalen said,
" if he'll promise to come home before
Christmas."

Otho h'md and ha'd, and said at last, he
could not promise more than she did. He
would do his best too.

" It would be very nice," Magdalen said
reflectively. " Bradstane *is* dull to the
carnally minded. People given up to good
works and acts of mercy, like Miss Askam,
may find it bearable. I think it is awful.
And there is hardly any one left in it now.
All my old friends are gone. You away,
Otho ; Gilbert away ; Roger Camm gone."

" Camm lives in Leeds now, doesn't he ? "
asked Otho ; and there was something in
his voice as he spoke—an inflexion, a
shade, which caused Eleanor to glance at

him quickly. But he looked as usual, except that he was still haggard and worn-looking, and appeared indifferent about the answer.

"Yes," said his sister. "He has a very good post there."

"What has become of that little girl he was going to marry?" asked Otho; and Magdalen gave a little laugh, saying—

"Well, that is good, I must say. After the way you behaved to her——"

"What?" stammered Otho, and there was the same look on his face that Eleanor had seen there as he stood in the hall just before Magdalen's arrival.

"He pretends not to know," said Magdalen mockingly. "It is not a hundred years since there was a concert in the Bradstane schoolroom, sir."

And she laughed her measured, cold laugh.

"Oh, bah!"

"Ada Dixon was very much out of health,

and was sent away into Devonshire into a warmer climate," said Eleanor gravely. "She has been away all the summer, and has not yet returned."

"Ah!" said Otho, stifling a yawn. "I used to see her in former days, going up and down the village, and going to see you, Mag——"

"Yes. You put a stop to that by your behaviour that night. After that it was impossible for me to have anything more to do with her."

He laughed.

"I never saw anything of her this time, so I thought she might have got married to some one, and cleared out."

Neither his sister nor Magdalen saw how, as he spoke, he looked sideways at them. Magdalen was opening and shutting her fan. Eleanor had some trifle of fancy work in her hands.

He did not stay much longer, but had some talk with Magdalen at the door before he went away. He did not wait till Miss Strangforth's carriage came, nor offer, as on a former occasion, to see her home. Magdalen returned to Eleanor when the door had closed behind Otho.

" He is really exasperating. He will not give me his address now ; says he is so uncertain : I must write through Gilbert, as usual. I declare he grows more and more mysterious. One might almost think he had some reason for wishing to conceal his whereabouts," Magdalen went on reflectively. " Suppose one wanted to get at him suddenly, in any emergency, and everything had to be done through Gilbert. It might be most awkward."

She spoke with entire tranquility of mien and voice, and stood before the looking-glass over the mantelpiece, arranging the flowers in her corsage, with drooped eye-lids and leisurely fingers. It was evidently a purely imaginary picture that she drew. But Eleanor looked up sharply, remembering what she had witnessed that very evening. Magdalen, however, was no person to whom she could disclose her vague and shadowy fears. There was nothing for it but silence. She gave a troubled sigh.

.

CHAPTER IX.

THE RETURN.

With Otho's absence and silence, the uneasiness and the fears which he seemed to
bring with him, like so many invisible but
potent attendants, gradually died away and
were lulled into serenity. The great house
was closed. The Thorsgarth shooting was
let, so Eleanor heard. She never went
near the place, and heard nothing of it all.
Her own life was sweet to her just now,
and full of hope. The most beautiful
season of the year floated by like an
ideal, a dream of peace and of calm, yet
ample life.

It would be almost impossible to imagine

anything more beautiful than the aspect of
Teesdale—especially of that portion of
Teesdale—in the months of September
and October—when they are fine and
seasonable, that is, and bring such skies,
such winds, and such suns as are due, in
these two most gorgeous months of the
year.

In this particular season they were all
that could be desired, and our lovers—for
lovers they were, though no explicit word
of love had ever passed between them
—enjoyed their glory to their heart's
content. Eleanor was satisfied that
Michael did not speak to her; the spell
of the present time was so delicious that
she would not have had it broken.
She had forgotten outside troubles and
difficulties; she only felt that all was well,
and that a happiness awaited her in the
future, so great that she could well afford
to wait for it.

September sighed itself out in golden

glory, leaving a luxury of ripening tints
on every tree, filling the tangled hedges
with many-coloured flames of dying weeds ;
for, as every one knows who lives in the
country, the smaller plants that grow in
the ditches and near to the ground—the
wild geranium, the smaller hemlock, or
that plant which is akin to it, the rose-
bushes, the hawthorn, and wild guelder
rose—these are the things that " turn "
first, these the objects on which autumn
first places her crimson finger ; and then,
when she has embellished the hedges, and
is pleased with the result of her handi-
work, she becomes bolder, mounts higher,
attacks the trees—the oak and the beech
first, the sycamore and the ash following
in their turn. Then it is that the river
gains his stronger voice, and rushes along,
ever more tumultuously. Then it is that
o' nights the air is keen, and that at that
hour which has said good-bye to afternoon,
and is not yet evening, there is a strange

metallic, lambent light in the sky, a light
which seems also almost to crackle and
sparkle in the very atmosphere, a magic,
unearthly light, which has its charms for
those who love to study nature in her more
obscure phases.

It was on a glorious crisp afternoon, a
little beyond the middle of October, that
Eleanor returned to the Dower House,
after driving about a bevy of little Johnsons the whole afternoon. She dressed
herself then, and went to dine and spend
the evening at the old doctor's house.
After dinner Michael came in. He
seemed lately to have enjoyed an unusual
quantity of leisure in the evening hours.
The talk turned to books ; amongst other
books to a book of poetry, some passage
in which was disputed. Eleanor said that
she had the book, and would go across to
her house and fetch it. Upon this Michael
announced that he should convey her
across the square, and had gone as far as

the door of the doctor's house with her, when his old friend, who was in his library, called to him, hearing his step.

"Go to him," said Eleanor. "I will fetch the book, and return to you." And she walked quickly across the square to her own door.

Arrived there, she found a woman's figure standing, in an uncertain attitude, near it. Something—a nameless chill, an unspeakable dread, took possession of her. She did not speak, but paused, looking at the figure, her mind disturbed with vague recollections of Otho's last visit, and of the disagreeable dream she had had months ago, concerning him.

"Miss Askam!" said the loiterer, in an uncertain voice.

"Yes ; who is it ?"

"It is I—Ada. I wanted to speak to you."

"Come in with me, then," she replied, but felt all the time that she was inviting

some great terror and woe to enter her
house.

She opened the door, and led Ada into
the drawing-room, turned up the light, and
looked at her; and as she looked, the
words were frozen upon her lips at the
aspect of the figure before her. Had not
the voice said, " It is I—Ada," she would
scarcely have recognized this countenance.
Ada wore a large, thick, woollen shawl,
falling loosely about her; and a small hat,
from under which showed a face which
had aged by twenty years, and which was
not only aged, but seamed, furrowed, worn
with lines of what must have been mortal
anguish, seeing that every one of them
had been stamped in less than five short
months. The pretty, delicate, meaning-
less face was clean gone : in its stead
there was a mask, betraying a mind de-
voured by misery; eyes which looked at
once hard and frightened, hunted and yet
defiant—the eyes of an animal at bay; a

countenance to fill the most indifferent beholder with horror.

Struck literally speechless, Eleanor stood, her hand on the table, and stared at the figure with wide open eyes, while she felt cold and terror seize every limb. What did this apparition want with her or hers ? A sickly dread, a kind of dim first suspicion of the meaning of it all crept into her heart.

"Miss Askam," said this spectre of Ada Dixon, in a low and husky voice, " I'm in trouble."

" Yes," almost gasped the other.

"I'm come to you, since it was no use writing to your brother. Where is he ? "

The tongue of Eleanor at first clave to the roof of her mouth ; at last, in a hoarse voice, she asked—

"What have you to do with my brother?"

With a swift motion, Ada unfastened the pin at her throat; her shawl slid from her shoulders to the ground, and she confronted Eleanor.

Trembling overpowered the latter. Speech was at first denied her. She could stand no more, but crouched upon a chair, and gasped out—

" Oh, horrible, horrible ! "

Suddenly a wild gleam of hope crossed her mind. Why was she assuming the very worst to have happened ? By what right did she condemn not only Otho, but Ada ? She sprang up again, went close to the girl, and almost whispered—

" Did he not marry you ? "

" Marry me ! " repeated Ada, in a fearful voice of bitterness, scorn, and despair. " Nay, he only swore he would, again and again."

" And—and——" she shivered still. " And when was this ? "

" It was in March," replied Ada, with stony composure. " When I was staying in Wensleydale, and he was in Friarsdale,

and he met me every day, and said he'd
never cared for anybody else. I've written
to him—a hundred letters. He has never
answered one. I thought he was at home
now; I heard so. I came to tell him he
must—to shame him, if I couldn't persuade
him; and now . . . he's not here. No
one knows . . . where he is."

With an hysterical sob she sank together
in the corner of a couch.

"In March," Eleanor was repeating to
herself, with mechanical calm, and clench-
ing her hands, to keep herself still.
"March—and this is October. There is
yet time."

That was all she could think of at the
moment. There was no time, no possibility for anything else. Her brain felt
wound up to this emergency, and to
nothing more. She walked up to Ada,
and touched her.

"Your parents—what do they know?"

"Nothing," said Ada, in a dull, colour-

less monotone. "Mother is away, or I
dare not have come home. Father is
away for the night. He'll be back to-
morrow : he will find out . . . he will
turn me out of doors. Oh, Miss Askam,
save me, save me, save me !"

"Hush !" said Eleanor quietly. "Let
me think. Some one must have known—
the people you were staying with—your
aunt ?"

"She would keep me no longer. I put
her off by telling her that he was coming
down there to marry me—that he'd sent
me there to wait for him. I said it all
depended on her keeping silence ; that
was why she let me stay so long."

"At what time will your father be
back ?"

"At eleven to-morrow morning, they
said."

"You will go home now, and stay there
all night. At nine o'clock to-morrow
morning come to me. I shall have had

time to make arrangements then. I will
see your father. I do not think he will
turn you out of doors. If he does,
you shall come here. I will send for—
my brother. I think I can make him
come. I do not wish to seem harsh
to you, but you must go home now,
that I may have time to arrange things.
You will go to your room at once, when
you get home. You understand—you
can say you are tired. Try not to be
frightened," she added, bending over Ada,
who was crouched in an attitude of blank
despair; "because I can shelter you, and
I will do so, as God is above us. I
promise you this. Now go."

Slowly Ada rose. Eleanor felt afraid
lest she should break down before she
had left the house. But she did not.
She submitted to have her shawl pinned
on again, and with the same look of utter,
vacant despair, walked away.

" Either it will turn her brain or kill

her," Eleanor felt, as the girl departed,
and she sat down at the table, and rested
her head on her hands, and tried to put
away the recollection of the awful figure
she had seen, and to reflect upon what
must be done. But she scarcely had sufficient power yet, over her emotion, to be
able to reflect. She could only remember,
and shudder, and feel horrified, while all
kinds of wild speculations darted through
her mind, as to the effect the event would
have upon this person, and that person;
and, above all, she wondered how it was
that it had never for one moment occurred
to any of them that when Ada was·in
Wensleydale, and Otho in Friarsdale, they
might easily have met. In fact, she could
think of nothing but of the thing itself,
and the crushing, the overwhelming horror
of it, except that every now and then
a thought crossed her mind that something must be done at once, and that
there was no one but herself to do it;

which thought reduced her to complete powerlessness.

While she sat in this chaos of thought and emotion she heard a knock at the door. She said nothing; she had forgotten all about the little things that one remembers at ordinary times, and after a moment, while she still sat, unheeding, it was gently opened, and Michael Langstroth looked in.

"I have been sent to fetch you," he had begun, and then he came to a dead stop, as he saw and comprehended her strange attitude; and when, at his voice, she raised her head and looked at him, he beheld her face, and knew that since she had quitted them, a quarter of an hour ago, something terrible had happened to her. And he knew that moment—he did not in so many words state it to himself, but he knew it—that it was to him she would appeal for help. He was glad of that, but he was sorry that he had let the days

go by in a dream, and had not given her
the right to come to him, without thought
and without question.

Eleanor, as she looked at him, felt at
first a little bewildered. So overwhelmed
was she with what had passed, that it
was a moment or two before she actually
realized who he was.

" I will lift up mine eyes unto the hills,"
says the Psalmist, " from whence cometh
my help." And, in a certain degree, it was
so with her. A voice supreme and unerring spoke to her ; all her nature, every
fibre seemed to bow to an overwhelming
intuition which directed her towards the
man who stood before her, looking so
earnestly down upon her. She loved him,
and that with a love which had grown
into a great passion, and an absorbing
one. But it was something different—
something deeper and higher than even
this great love which impelled her action
now ;—instinct, some might call it, and

others say that she had naturally a gift
for reading character correctly, and for
discerning which persons were, and which
were not to be relied upon. She herself
would have said that God inspired her.
She sat motionless for a moment, bending
to this inner voice which spoke to her,
acknowledging what her belief told her
was the providential arrival of the one
person whom she would most implicitly
trust—and fighting down the unwilling-
ness—natural and good in itself, but which
she felt it was useless to stand upon now
—to speak openly of such things as had
happened, to a man who was neither her
husband, her father, nor her brother.
And then, her resolution taken, or rather,
that importunate inner voice obeyed, she
got up, and leaning over the table towards
him said—

"I want to know if you will help me in
a very great trouble?"

"With every power that I have, I will

help you," he replied unhesitatingly, and
waited to hear what it was that he had
to do.

"Since I came in I have heard of a
thing that has happened. I hardly know
how to tell you of it. It makes me feel
as if I had been laughing and amusing
myself in some room, underneath which
another person was being tortured to
death."

Her lips were parched ; her eyes
dilated.

"If I did not trust you *entirely*," she
said, as if she appealed to him, "I could
not tell you." •

For a moment she was silent, while
Michael waited, and then, turning to him
again, told him unfalteringly of the discovery she had made, and repeated, word
for word, the conversation between herself
and Ada. Michael listened in perfect
silence ; it was, he felt, the only way in
which to hear such a tale.

" I have sent her home," Eleanor said
at last, " that I might try to think. She
is safe for to-night, since she says her
mother is away, and her father will not
return before eleven to-morrow. I have
told her to come here early—at nine
to-morrow morning. I thought I would
keep her here till her parents knew.
I think her father has a heart, but I cannot endure that woman, her mother. I
feel that she would rail at her—not because
she had done wrong, but because she had
failed in getting married to Otho."

He nodded.

" Do you think I have done right ? "

" Perfectly right. There was nothing
else to be done. Do you know where—
he—is ? "

He spoke as if he found a difficulty in
finding a term by which to speak of Otho.

" No, I do not ; but your—Mr. Langstroth
knows all about him. He gave me his
address at Christmas, and I have kept it.

It is through him we shall have to send.
. . . It is now clear to me why Otho
would not give his address to Magdalen."

"I see. The thing is, suppose he does
not choose to answer the summons—your
brother, I mean. You say she said she
had written to him?"

"A hundred times, she said, and received
no answer."

"That looks very much as if he had
chosen to desert her entirely, and did not
intend to notice any demand. I fear he
will not come if we send for him."

"I do not know that. I think he may.
I have an idea in my mind. I will tell
you why I have it, afterwards. Since you
told me what his besetting sin was, I have
watched him carefully. He does what he
feels inclined to do, and leaves the results
to chance. I have seen it in a thousand
things, great and small. I can tell no
reason why he should have committed
this crime—his heart is black—I do not

understand such things. But I believe
that when last he saw the girl, he did not
know of this, and that he was tired of the
caprice, and afraid that her letters might
tell him of some such thing; so he has
never read them, but trusted to his god,
chance, that they did not tell him what he
did not want to hear. I saw him burn a
thing one day, without opening it. Your
brother asked him why he did that, when
he knew it was a bill he would have to
pay. He said he knew nothing till he
had read it."

She also told him of the episode she had
seen between Otho and the young woman
who had been singing.

"The expression on his face was fear,'
she went on, as coolly as she could. "I
did not understand it then. Now I do.
It was dusk. He could not see the
figure properly; he feared to meet Ada;
he thought for a moment that it was Ada,
come to accuse him of his sin. All the

time he was here he must have been
haunted by the fear that she might con-
front him. His questions to us about her,
were for a blind; and I think he wanted
to get some news of her, without seeming
to seek it. As we told him nothing, he
chose to behave as if there were nothing
to tell. This has all come into my mind
since I have seen Ada. Perhaps I am
wrong; but if I am right—and I believe I
am, and we send a message to Mr. Gilbert
Langstroth, Otho will know what it means,
and will come."

"Could Gilbert have known?"

"No, no, no!" she exclaimed vehemently. "I will stake my life on it that
he did not."

"I think your theory may be quite right,
up to a certain point. You may be right
as to the past, that is, for that would be
quite consistent with his character. But
I doubt your sanguine anticipations being
correct. I doubt his coming, if we send

for him. Suppose he is out of England, and refuses to come ; because it would be so much easier for him just to leave her to you, or to herself, or to her fate."

" There is some little time yet. If he does not answer, I will go to him where he is, and make him come. I will so speak to him that he shall not dare do anything but come. I will die, but I will force him to make what miserable reparation lies with him. He is poor now," she added, with a peculiar smile, such as Michael had never seen upon her face before. " Before very long, he will be a pauper. I know it. He will be dependent upon me. I have understood that for some little time past. But if he does not come home and marry Ada, I will let him die of hunger in the street, rather than give him a penny."

She did not speak noisily nor vehemently, but Michael saw that she was quite prepared to carry out her words.

"Then you have a strong hold upon him," he said. "Now, what we have to do, is to telegraph to Gilbert. We can, of course, have an answer from him to-morrow. By the way, it cannot go before to-morrow. Then we shall know better what to do. If you will give me pen and paper, we can perhaps agree together what to say."

Eleanor brought the writing things, and after various false attempts, they decided to send :—

"Send O. A. here instantly, on a matter of life and death. Not an hour to be lost. If he is not near, send information how he is soonest to be found."

"I will see that it goes first thing in the morning," said he. "And you say Ada is coming to you?"

"Yes; at nine."

"That is well. She could not be in a better place. Do not leave your house yourself. I will see Mr. Dixon. There is no necessity for you to trouble. Try to make her talk to you about it; do you understand ? It will be better for her than anything. It may save her life and her reason."

"Yes, I will do so. Do you think I should send for her here to-night?"

"No, I do not. It would excite the curiosity and suspicion of your own servants, and the tale would be over the whole village long before morning. I shall be obliged to tell them over the way, though," he added, "because it might be just possible that Gilbert's reply might make it necessary for some one to go up to town, to settle things more expeditiously. I might go up alone; or if you went, I would go with you—if I may."

"If you may!" she repeated, in a faltering voice. "What could *I* have done without you!"

"Another time," said he, looking straight into her eyes, "I will tell you something.

We have other things to think about now. Be as tranquil as you can, and remember that you could have done nothing but what you have done."

He wrung her hand without saying anything more, and left her.

They had searched their hearts to find what was the best to do in this terrible emergency, and being at one on the point they did it. The time in which to decide was short, and they did not know the whole extent of the woe about which they were, as it were, legislating. Perhaps they tacitly agreed that the nature which had endured so long could endure till to-morrow morning. They knew not what were the principal factors in the sum of the events, in the midst of which they found themselves without a moment's warning. Those factors were despair, and the promptings of a heart which had literally had all life and all reason ground out of it by seven months of perfect wretchedness.

Eleanor slept little that night, and waited with sickening anxiety for nine o'clock. It came, but brought not Ada with it. Half-past nine; yea, ten had struck, and she came not. Thrilling with uneasiness, Eleanor knew not what to do. She feared by making inquiries to excite suspicion. Unhappy and uncertain, she waited till about half-past ten. Michael called, and, without sitting down, just told her not to make herself more uneasy than was necessary, but that he had been at Mr. Dixon's, intending to appoint a meeting with him on his return. His assistant said he had had a letter from him, deferring his return till the following day, and that the maid had told him that Miss Dixon had gone out, and up the town, without waiting for any breakfast.

Eleanor felt her heart in her mouth.

" Has she gone out to kill herself ? " she whispered.

" I do not think so," said Michael. " She

cannot have wandered very far. You shall have news as soon as I can send it. There is only one road out of this end of the town, and I am riding that way. Good morning."

So she was left alone, with the conviction that Michael himself was far more disturbed than he chose to tell her. Fears and terrors loomed up like giant shadows in the background of her mind, and so she passed the most terrible day of her life.

CHAPTER X.

ADA.

ADA had gone home, after leaving the Dower House. The maid had told Michael that Miss Dixon had gone out about eight o'clock, in her bonnet and shawl, without any breakfast, and that she had had nothing to eat after her arrival at home. She had never, indeed, taken her things off; but was in exactly the same dress she had worn on her journey to Bradstane, which had been a long and fatiguing one. On going home from her interview with Eleanor, she went upstairs, partly in mechanical obedience to a remembered mandate of Miss Askam's, partly automatically.

She never undressed, or even lay down on her bed. Part of the cruel night she spent in sitting on a chair by the wall, staring with blank eyes into the darkness, and repressing, half mechanically, the moans that rose to her lips. Another portion of her vigil was consumed in a restless wandering to and fro. Her chamber was over the empty parlour. No one would hear or heed her footsteps. At last, finding the darkness unbearable, she struck a match, and lighted two candles which stood on the dressing-table, and gazed about the room. It was her own bedroom that she was in, and the bed, beside which she sat, was the bed in which Ada Dixon had slept—the same Ada Dixon who had felt indignant and insulted when her plain-spoken lover had told her that no honest girl required notice from her superiors. How very angry she had been when he said it. At this recollection she held her hands before her mouth to stifle a shriek. In this room, before that looking-glass, how many hours had she spent, trying the effect of this, that, or the other piece of finery; endeavouring to model her bonnets, her hats, her mantles, and her gowns upon those of her patroness, Magdalen Wynter? In that desk, standing upon the little round table in the corner, how many notes might be reposing, indited by Otho Askam? Notes slipped into her hand under Magdalen's very eyes, when he had met her at Balder Hall; behind her unsuspecting father's back, when she happened to be in the shop. Notes containing at first nothing but a rather heavy style of compliment, adapted to a taste not over-fastidious in such matters; tragic effusions, when read by the light of this present; ponderously comic, if viewed critically on their intrinsic merits as compositions.

When had it first seriously occurred to her that she might become Mrs. Askam, of Thorsgarth? Why, on that night, a hundred years ago, when there had been a grand concert, at which she had sung— when Miss Wynter had been flouted, and Ada flattered and complimented.

That was the night Roger had come in in such a fury, and carried her away. Roger—Roger—her thoughts wandered— who was Roger, and what had he to do with her? They were engaged to be married once—now—yet—— Yes, and in November he was to come and see her.

Again a scream of wild laughter rose to her lips. Again she managed to stifle it, and again her mind reverted, whether she would or no, to her horror, her nightmare, the history of the last seven months. She recollected how Otho had appeared one day at the farmhouse where she was staying, and had paid her compliments; how she, grown bolder now that Magdalen was not present to overawe her, had, in a perkish manner, chaffed him about his engagement; to which he had retorted that he was not married yet, and that engagements might be broken off; and had appealed to her admiring cousins to know if Miss Dixon would not grace any sphere, even the most exalted. She remembered the gradually arising passion in his looks and his words, and how she herself, by one of those mysterious attractions which we see daily exemplified, had found herself spellbound by him in a manner which Roger could never have compassed if he had died for it. Temptation, kisses, promises—such profuse promises, appealing with instinctive acuteness to her vanity, her love of distinction —the strange eyes which magnetized and fascinated her; a brief, delirious dream— and since then, hell, by day and by night; not from the sense of defilement which would kill some natures—but, let the truth be written of her; she has her compeers in many places—from the scorching conviction that if, or when, she was found out, disgrace and contumely would be her portion.

She recalled the parting from Roger— when she had dismissed him in the pride of her heart, at a time when hope was still strong; and though she was beginning to have sickening qualms, yet she had been deluded enough to mistake his footstep behind her for Otho's, and had had a wild idea that he had at last broken with Magdalen, and was coming to save and to claim her. Then her departure ; the letters she had written, which had never been noticed ; her aunt's gradually awakened suspicions, and the tales she had told to stave off ruin and discovery ; her journey home in fluttering hope, and desperate resolve ; for a letter from home in which her father had expressed himself obscurely, had made her think Otho was at Thorsgarth. How she had made inquiries, and learnt that he had been gone a month or more. Then

Eleanor, and her promises, and how she was to go and see her in the morning.

The night hours passed swiftly in this consuming vigil, and presently Ada saw that it was broad day, time, therefore, to go and see Miss Askam. That was her one thought now, that she was to go and see Miss Askam. And yet, her mind being more than a little wandering, she did not realize that though daylight, it was not yet the appointed time; but went downstairs, and let herself out of the house. The maid was at work in the kitchen; but she was a new-comer since Ada had left home, and did not therefore address her, or ask her any questions.

When Ada was out in the street she felt very weak and very strange, but she looked at a clock which stood over a public building, nearly opposite her father's house. The hands pointed to eight; and then she remembered vaguely that Miss Askam had said nine; she must not go before nine.

She would take a little walk then, in the early freshness; she could not go back to that dreadful room. Besides, she had advanced a little up the town, into the square: there were Miss Askam's blinds still down; it would not do to go there yet, though she longed to do so, and, had she been in her right mind, would have knocked without further ado, confident in the generous charity of the other woman.

So she wandered on, out of the town, faint and feeble for want of food and rest; crazy, and growing every moment more so, with woe, and fear, and wretchedness. Soon she was on a lonely road, stretching out to the north-east, with few houses, and, at that hour, scarcely a person on it. How beautiful it all was, in this golden morning sunshine, with the mists rising from the river, and the trees, clad in yellow and scarlet and russet, heavy and drooping in the windless air of a frosty October morning, precursor of a glorious autumn day!

Then she emerged from the shade of these trees, and found herself upon a wild upland road, with sweeps of country stretching far and wide around her; fields of yellow stubble, pastures, meadows; stretches of heavy wood; here and there the gleam of the river, and on every side, the wall of blue fells in the distance. The rough, uphill road lay before her, with scarce a house to be seen; and overhead a blue sky, from which fleecy white clouds were everywhere rolling back to show the fathomless, serene expanse.

"Ay, but I'm so tired, so tired!" Ada sighed, as she stumbled, and then recovered herself. "This is not being a lady; why does he not come home? If I had the carriage he promised me,—he said he would drive to Balder Hall with me, to see Miss Wynter, and show her what *he* thought of me, when we were married."

Here she found herself opposite to a tiny house at the roadside, or rather, at a corner where four roads met ; and at its door a woman stood, saw her, called out to her, and wished her good day.

"Good day!" said Ada, with a sudden affectation of her old mincing manner. " Might I beg a drink of water from you ? "

The woman, who was kindly, though rough, would have had her come in and have some bread and milk, but she would not. She had quite forgotten Eleanor Askam by this time, and said she had far to go, and must not wait. The water was bestowed upon her, and she stood to drink it, holding the cup with her right hand, while her left rested upon the table. The woman looked at her, and drew her own conclusions from what she saw. Ada thanked her, with an affectation of superiority and patronage, and left the cottage. Its mistress stood watching her, as she turned to the right, along a high, toilsome road, and marched slowly and heavily along it.

"Some poor crazy creature, whose hour
is not far off. God pity her!" she said
within herself, and for a moment felt
inclined to run after the girl, and insist on
sheltering her. But the thought of her
" man," and the trouble he would feel it to
have such a person in the house deterred
her. She went inside again, to her morning's work.

Ada crept on, till she saw at a little
distance, gray farm-buildings and a white-
washed house, with a long, low front ; and
it came across her mind that she could not
walk any further, but that she would go
there, and ask them to let her rest till her
carriage came, which was to meet her
there, and take her home to lunch. And
if they asked her who she was—why,
the answer was simple—Mrs. Askam, of
Thorsgarth. And in fancy, she saw
curtseys dropped, and heard them begging
her to be seated. For she was now quite
crazy, only in this way; the connecting

string in all her wild thoughts, was the vague recollection of real promises.

Before she arrived at the farm, she swerved to one side; her knees gave way, and in a little hollow in the wall, where there was a heap of stones, she sank down, feeling as if she were going to sleep; but the sleep became a long, deadly faint, and Ada Dixon, the petted beauty of the old town where she had been born and bred, who had been the plighted wife of a good man, lay in a heap by the roadside, with only the broad sky above her, with nothing but her mother earth on which to rest her dainty limbs.

And here she continued to lie, till Michael Langstroth rode up, having made inquiries on his way, and learnt from the woman at the cross-roads, that such a young woman as he described had passed.

"Ay, doctor," said the woman, who knew him, though not Ada. "She was none fit to be walking on such roads at such

times. I wanted her to bide a bit, and
rest; but nay—she said she had far to go,
and yon's t' rooad she took."

Michael rode on, determined to find her,
for Roger's sake, for the sake of Eleanor,
and out of his own pity for her condition.
He was not long in coming within sight
of the gray stone farm, and within a stone's
throw of it, the curve in the wall, and the
figure that lay beneath it.

He muttered an inarticulate word, as
he sprang from his horse, and stooped over
her, and when he saw her face, recoiled
for a moment. For a brief instant or two
he could see nothing distinctly, a film was
over his eyes, and a great sob in his throat,
as he turned, and hung his horse's bridle
over the post of a gate in the wall. He
then stooped down, raised the lifeless
figure in his arms, and carried her over
the rough road to the farm door. The
dogs, who were his friends, came out to
welcome him, and then stopped, sniffing

suspiciously at the skirts of the strange burden he bore. The farmer's wife saw him, and ran forward, with upraised hands, " Lord 'a mercy, Doctor Langstroth—what is't ? "

" Mrs. Nadin, you have promised many a time to do me a good turn ; and I want a very good one doing now. Give a shelter to this poor thing till her trouble is over ; it is a sad tale, and I'll tell it you afterwards."

Mrs. Nadin made no more ado. Langstroth had, according to her, saved her husband's life two years ago, and with true north country love, she had been ever since burning to " pay him back again." She only stopped to look at the girl's face, and to ejaculate Ada's name. Then she called her daughter to her aid, and they whispered horror-struck conjectures to one another as they tended the wretched young woman.

And here, under the roof of these pitiful strangers was that evening born, before his time, the son of Otho Askam—a child of sorrow, if ever one came into the world.

CHAPTER XI.

THE BROTHERS.

IT was late in the evening of the same day. Eleanor and Michael were alone together in her drawing-room. She had not been left alone all day. Unable to bear the solitude and suspense alone, she had sent for Mrs. Parker who, of course, knew all the story from Michael. The good lady had come, and remained with her during all the hours of waiting and terror. When Michael was announced, Eleanor had said she would like to see him alone, and Mrs. Parker had gone into another room. He had come in, looking both tired and haggard; for what had

happened had struck him, both through
his friend, and through the woman he
loved. Though Roger had now no
connection with Ada, Michael knew him
too well to suppose for a moment that
he had, or could have ceased to love
her, in the space of five short months.
The worst agony of separation might
be over, but he could imagine what
this news would be to the man who had
loved this unhappy girl so tenderly and so
faithfully. As for Eleanor, her sufferings
were his sufferings now. And thirdly,
there was himself and his own sensations
in the matter. He had never admired
Ada, and had always been sorry that she
had been Roger's choice; but it had never
entered into his head to dream of such a
dénouement to the broad farce he had seen
played at the concert. It was not that he
had credited Otho with being any better
than he was, but it had not occurred to
him to look at such a side as being possible

to the affair. If any one had suggested
it to him, he would have said first, that
Otho would not dare to commit such a
sin where a girl of Ada's upbringing was
concerned, and next, that Ada herself was
beyond suspicion. The whole thing had
burst upon him, and he was filled with
disgust and horror, such as a man whose
mind and life have been alike clean, must
feel when he comes face to face with such
a history, and finds it intruding itself into
the most intimate relations of his own
life.

Summoning up his courage, he had told
her all that had happened. She had at
first been standing. As he proceeded, her
face went paler; her limbs trembled. At
the picture of how he had found Ada lying
by the roadside, the tears rained from her
eyes. And when he ceased to speak she
was seated at the table, her head buried in
her arms, as if she would fain have hidden
her face from him and from all the world.

Indeed, a cloud of great darkness hung over her soul, and it seemed for the moment as if neither religion nor hope, nor any good thing could stand in the presence of overwhelming, triumphant villainy like this.   Michael was watching her silently, while a conflict was going on in his own mind.   She considered him the embodiment of strength and goodness, and believed implicitly in a most godlike mind which she attributed to him.   And he knew she thought that of him.   Women's eyes have the habit of confiding such opinions, to the men concerning whom they hold them, when their tongues may not say the same things.   Michael knew very well that he was nothing at all like what she imagined him to be ; indeed, he perhaps would not have been what she thought him if he could.   He was, as he knew, something a great deal more serviceable and useful in this working day world —a man, with a man's wants and failings and weaknesses. And the desire which just then was stronger in him than anything else was, not to lecture this young woman, from the superior standpoint of a godlike intelligence, on the futility of her cries and tears, but to clasp her in his arms, and tell her that it was all very dreadful—even more dreadful than she in her innocence knew or could understand yet, and that he only asked her to let him take the half of all her trouble upon himself. That was his impulse, even as he stood here. And the conflicting agency, which beat back this desire was, the fear lest to do what he wished now might bear the semblance of entrapping her, of taking her unawares, and of making her need into his opportunity. Not very godlike this, nor very superior, but quite human.

"All is of no use, then?" she said at last, raising her face, tear-stained and disfigured, from her hands, and looking at him. Then, as if a sudden thought had struck her, she rose and came hastily near to where he stood.

"How stupid of me to sit crying there, and thinking of nothing but myself, while *you* think of every one except yourself. You wish me to go to her, do you not? And I will go. I will be ready directly, if you will wait. I never thought of it. If he deserts her, I will not. If I can do nothing else, I can sit by her, and people can hear that I am there. That is always something."

She made a step as if to go to the door. Michael caught her hand to detain her.

"No, no! I was thinking nothing of the kind," said he. "You must not go. Do you know—but of course you don't—that she is perfectly insane at this present moment? She would not know you. She does not know me; and she would shriek with horror if any one showed her her child. She is in the right hands, and you must not go near her."

" Mad—but she will get better ? "

"I hope so—at least, perhaps she may."

" But she will recover her reason ? "

" Most likely, if she lives. But it may be a long time first."

Stayed in her desire to go to Ada's help, and as it were cast back upon herself, Eleanor stood drooping for a moment.

" Have you had no telegram from London ? " he asked.

" Oh, I had nearly forgotten. This is it," she said, taking it from the mantelpiece. Michael read—

" Your message received and attended to." It was from Gilbert. He turned.it over reflectively.

" H'm ! I wonder what that means."

" Can it mean that he is coming ? I wish he had been more explicit."

" He would not wish to excite suspicion. Bradstane suspicion is easily aroused. If he did come, it would be by the south mail, which is due in a quarter of an hour.

If you like, if you will allow me, I will wait with you till he comes ; or rather, till we see whether he comes."

"You are very good. You are sure there is nothing more that I can do ? "

" Nothing, at present."

" Then shall we go to the other room, and stay with Mrs. Parker till we know what happens ? "

" If you like," said Michael slowly ; and he felt as if some living, tangible thing were rushing on wings of swiftness towards them, so visibly, to him, did the moment approach when the veil between them should be rent aside. Yet he made a step towards the door, as if to open it for her ; and she moved towards it too, and swerved unsteadily to one side, for excitement and suspense had told upon her and weakened her. Michael knew that she was proud, and that her pride impelled her to conceal what she felt as long as was practicable ; but not the slightest sign or

movement that she made could escape
him. He was at her side in an instant.

"No, stay here! Do not go into the
other room," he said, taking her hand.
"I will bring Mrs. Parker to you, if you
like; but do you stay here."

He had a firm hand, and a grasp at
once strong and gentle; and as she felt her
hand in it she paused again, steadying herself against the head of a sofa, and looking
at him, half-affrighted, half-eager, at the
look she encountered.

"It was nothing — the weakness of a
moment," she said. "I will conquer it. I
must not give way now."

"I think you must," said he, as he re-
leased her hand, and stood before her for
a moment. "You are faint; you are
weak; you are broken. This battle is
one for which you have never been trained.
Give way; it is the best."

"And what is to become of me if I
do?" she asked blankly.

Michael opened wide his arms. She looked at him for a little while, and then, with a low sobbing, as of one who is weary and broken-hearted, moved towards him as he towards her, and found her rest.

  *   *   *   *   *

They were still sitting together, when a ring sounded through the house.

"That is just the time for the people from the south to come in," said Eleanor. And in another moment her maid had ushered Gilbert Langstroth into the room. Both of them noticed the expression upon Gilbert's face as he came in. It was one of eager expectancy. Both saw the glance which fell from his eyes upon Eleanor. It chilled her; it was like the looks he had bestowed upon her when he had sent her the flowers, before he had preached to her a sermon on the necessity of evil to the development of good in the world. But from her, his eyes fell upon Michael, and his face changed. He was quite silent. She rose, looking at him tremulously.

"You are very, very good. I did not quite know what to expect from your message," said she.

"I knew you would not. I could not explain in a telegram. From yours, I gathered that some kind of storm had burst, and that you were in trouble."

"I am in such trouble, that but for him," she said slowly, and stopped a moment, laying her hand upon Michael's arm, and looking very earnestly at Gilbert, who had gone very pale. Michael had not changed. But as Eleanor paused, Gilbert's eager look all faded, and he shook slightly from head to foot. The two brothers were regarding one another; for the first time for six years they were actually confronted. They must, to carry this business through, have some kind of intercourse and communication.

"But for him," she went on, "I could have done nothing. I—a woman, could have done nothing to any purpose."

She looked from one to the other of them earnestly, imploringly, and still there was silence; till at last she sat down at the table, rested her arms upon it, and leaning forward said, first to one and then to the other—

" Michael, you have spent your strength and your time this day in helping those who have never done you any good, in trying to save them from the effects of their sins, at least. And you, Gilbert, have come promptly here on no selfish errand. At my call you have come quickly to help me, who have no claim at all upon you. So good, and so considerate and helpful to others, will you go on hating each other; will you not be brothers again ? "

The two men were looking into each other's eyes, and Michael at last knew what that strange, potent sensation had been, which had shaken him on encountering Gilbert's look that night, when they

had been almost side by side at the con-
cert-room.   Not hate, not resentment, as
he had fancied; neither one nor the other;
but his old love for his brother, the
ancient, inborn love, which not all the
anger, enmity, and bitterness had succeeded in quenching.   And the voice
which addressed them both, went on
speaking still, earnestly, tremulously, with
passionate conviction—

"If but one good thing came out of
all this blackness, would it not be better
than nothing—nothing but sin and sorrow?
And there is so much grief and so much
wrong in the world, that if men had not
forgiveness to fight them with, I do not
see how there could be any chance for
happiness at all."

There was another little pause.   At last
Gilbert said, in a low voice—

"I never hated him——"

Without quite knowing how, they found
their hands clasped, each in one of the

other's, and Michael said, " Shall it be all over, Gilbert ? "

" From the bottom of my heart."

" Then let us say no more about it."

Eleanor rose.

" I shall leave you," she said gently. " Stay here if you choose. I shall go to Mrs. Parker."

Gilbert and Michael both made a movement towards the door, but something in Gilbert's look caused Michael to fall back and yield place to his brother. He turned away, went inside the room again, and looked into the fire, feeling that he could afford to be very magnanimous.

Gilbert opened the door, and as Eleanor was passing out, he said to her almost in a whisper—

" Only one word. You and he—are you—has he—have you given him any promise ? "

Eleanor looked at him steadily, though without any of the old distrust, and then answered him in the same voice, but with a proud smile—

" I have promised him everything. I have given my life into his hands."

" I am too late ? "

She hesitated, looking troubled. Gilbert smiled slightly.

" I should always have been too late, Eleanor ? "

She looked at him appealingly, and inclined her head. He bowed to her, and she went quickly away. Gilbert returned to the room, and to his brother.

" I shall never want to say anything to her again, Michael, that you may not hear."

Michael looked at him, but said nothing, and Gilbert went on—

" Shall we have to see her again to-night—on this matter, I mean ? "

" No. Let us go to my house, if you will come. There is a black business to be settled, sooner or later."

CHAPTER XII.

" AMIDST THE BLAZE OF NOON."

MICHAEL took his brother home, and so true is it that time and life can and do, if not wipe out, yet blur and deface the recollection of the sternest and most terrible past scenes, that Michael never once thought, as he opened the door, and ushered Gilbert in, of how that door had last closed upon his companion. Gilbert, however, remembered it — remembered many other things too, as he entered the familiar square hall, and looked furtively round at the well-known things which still furnished it. When they got into the library, some recollection of it all seemed to come to Michael too. Perhaps something in his brother's attitude, and in the slow, stiff way in which he moved and gazed about him, recalled past scenes to his mind. He turned to Gilbert, took his hand into one of his, and laid the other upon his shoulder.

"Gilbert, we have little time for going into old troubles, in the midst of these new ones; but, I say, let byegones be byegones. I am more glad than I can tell you to see you here; and I would like you to feel it your home again, if you can."

Gilbert's only present reply—though he had more to say, at some future date—was to wring the hand that held his. They understood each other again, at last—or, perhaps, for the first time; and as Michael said, there was no time for further explanations. He rang the bell, and ordered refreshments for his brother; and while Gilbert ate and drank, Michael sat conning over a railway guide, and jotting down memoranda.

"How long can you stay, Gilbert? Over to-morrow?"

"I could manage till the day after, if I wire to my head man to-morrow morning."

"That is well. Then to-morrow, I will leave you in charge here, and go over to Leeds, and tell Roger of this. If I began to write it, I should make a mess of it, I know; besides, writing is cold-blooded work, in such a case."

"It was all off between them, was it not?"

"Ay. But it never need have been, but for that d—d scoundrel philandering round the girl, and putting her out of conceit with Roger. It is his doing from beginning to end, and I must say I should glory in seeing him punished as he deserves. I think he wants tearing to pieces. But don't talk to me about it, or I shall lose all my self-control, and I want it every bit."

With which he returned to the study of Bradshaw, trying to make out how

he could soonest get himself conveyed
to Leeds, see Roger, and return to
Bradstane. And as he searched in the
railway guide, to see how the trains were
connected on the different lines, there came
into his mind a keen sense of the grimness
of the contrast between his errand, and the
means by which he was going to hurry to
Roger with his budget of ill-news, and
back again.

Our modern contrivances, indeed, for
speedily moving about from place to place,
and for darting news hither and thither,
have a certain appearance of haste and
want of dignity when tragedy comes in
question. And yet, it is surely a proof of
the intrinsic might, of the victorious power
of great elementary human emotions, that
when they are every now and then called
into play, in this decorous age, it is they
that triumph, and not the comfortable
arrangements which only take into account
ease of mind and plenty of purse. Love

and hate and despair go striding grimly or gloriously on, and live their lives, and strike their strokes, and sway the minds and souls of those possessed by them, and override . the obstacles in their course, as potently now as they did in more picturesque days. Bradshaw and the penny post come in in a parenthesis, and the system of electric tele-graphy powerfully supports them, so that we can send the news of our own cata-strophes, or of those of our neighbours, with a speed unheard of a century ago, though even before then there was a say-ing that " ill news travels fast." Nay, these things, if rightly considered, appear conducive to privacy rather than, as might appear from a superficial glance, to pub-licity. For any one who reads a startling announcement in letter or newspaper, has the habit, nowadays, of calling it a *canard*, and of saying that it is sure to be contra-dicted to-morrow. And so it often is. But even if it be not, this beautiful system

of Bradshaw, penny post and Co., has no
sooner certified the truth of one calamity,
than it is ready and to the fore with another,
and a worse than the former one ; which
second tragedy an intelligently interested
public devours, even if incredulous, with
never-satiated delight; and thus the immediate actors in the events chronicled are in
reality left almost as much to themselves
and their own devouring emotions, as they
would have been before the steam-engine
was invented. The world has heard of
your domestic drama, that is true ; and its
details have been printed in every daily
paper throughout the kingdom. But the
day after, it is provided with something
much more remarkable than your twopenny-
halfpenny calamity, and has forgotten in a
week that it ever heard your name.

Some such train of thought was in
Michael's mind, as he paused to consider
the sequence in which he should arrange
his different tasks on the morrow. Gilbert's

voice broke in upon his reverie. He had risen, and stood with his back against the mantelpiece.

" Michael, it seems that you and Miss Askam 'understand each other,' as the phrase goes."

" Yes, we do," said Michael.

" I'll make a clean breast of it. Last year, I came down here with some curiosity to see this girl who had come and planted herself down with Otho. Knowing what he was, I was undecided whether she was very fast, or very silly. So I came pre- pared for a good deal of amusement. You need not glare at me in that way. I would bet something you had your own private bit of astonishment in the matter, too. Well, the very first time I saw her, I understood one thing—that she was neither fast nor silly, and the more I saw of her the more lost in astonishment I was. Do you remember that knight in ' The Faery Queene'—I forget which he was—who

came across a woman of her sort, and was
struck dumb by her goodness, till

> " ' He himself, long gazing thereupon,
>   At last fell humbly down upon his knee,
>   And of his wonder made religion.'

It was something like that with me ; and
in a very short time I had made up my
mind that she was the woman I would
marry, if I could only get her to take me.
And I had the best hopes in the world,
for Otho had begun to conduct himself
like a maniac, even then, and she speedily
found out that I was the only person who
had any control over him. Well, then
came that night of the concert ; a good
many things came about that night, it
seems to me. And when I saw you and
her in the same room together, and you
speaking to her, and her to you, I was
certain there was something of the kind
going on. Michael, I gave her up from that
moment. . . . And yet, when time went
on—it is nearly a year ago—and I heard

of nothing between you, I began to think that, perhaps, after all, you had decided to have nothing to do with one who belonged to *us*, and I began to have a little hope again. When I got her telegram this morning, I felt a good deal of hope, and I frankly confess I was not sorry to hear that she was in trouble. I hoped that I could so serve her that I should be able to ask for a reward; and the shape I proposed to give it was, that we should pension off Otho with her money—some of it, you know—and that she should come to me, and never be troubled any more—if she only would. But you had forestalled me; and since it is you, I submit; but if it had been anybody else—— "

He paused expressively. Michael was looking earnestly at him, a crowd of new emotions in his heart. This, then, was the secret of Gilbert's conduct which had so puzzled Eleanor.

" I should have told her long ago that

I loved her," observed Michael ; "but there was her money, and her connections. They were too much for me."

"As far as money goes, you will be her equal," said Gilbert. "I don't suppose she will let Otho starve, and I can assure you there will not be a great superfluity of means when his affairs are wound up ; and now that this girl and this child will have to be provided for—— "

"If they live," put in Michael.

"If they live—yes. Well, that will make a hole in her income, I can assure you. While, on your part, there is that money—Michael —— " he hesitated, stammered—"that money that——"

"I know," said Michael quietly. "What about it?"

"Why, I have done well with it. I have always hoped that some day you would not reject it. It is six years ago, and I have made the most of it. It is a good large sum now—larger than if—— "

Michael gave a short laugh.

" I can well believe that."

" And if I am to believe that you have forgiven," he added earnestly, " you will not refuse any longer to take your share— ay, and as much more as you like—so that you can go to her and fear nothing, even if she loses every penny she has."

There was a pause. Michael at last said—

" You must let me think about it. I cannot decide such a thing all in a minute."

Indeed, he felt that he could not. And he was beginning to feel that six years ago he had been hard—as hard as some pagan or puritan, whose creed relentlessly demands an eye for an eye, and a tooth for a tooth. Quite a new feeling came over him with regard to Gilbert, who, it seemed, had worked for him for many years, and patiently bided till circumstances should allow him to offer the fruits of his work. Sweeping condemnations, he reflected, would be comfortable, very comfortable, to the carnal heart of offended man; but reasonable man must confess that scarcely ever are they just.

*　　*　　*　　*　　*

The months dragged on. Autumn fled by; winter had passed from off the face of the earth, and disappeared from the skies, but not from the soul and the mind of Ada. Gradually, after a long and terrible illness, her bodily health began to be restored. The death for which she had prayed, and which she had begged Michael wildly to procure for her, had stayed his hand. She was uplifted from the bed of sickness, but arose a changed being, altered and transformed apparently in her very nature. A melancholy, deep, black, and profound as the grave itself, had settled upon her. A melancholy which nothing ever seemed to move or change. She was not mad now, if she could still hardly be called sane, just because of this

black cloud which rolled between her and
other persons. She had no craze, and
no delusion, properly speaking; she was
simply dead to hope and joy, to every
amelioration of the present, to every hope
in the future. Eleanor studied her with
awe and wonder, realizing the mysterious
nature of the human creature in her. For
if Ada had lost great things, if she had
fallen from a high ideal, had been dashed
from a great height of purity and loftiness
of soul, and so had felt herself irreparably
stained and polluted, her present condition
of apathetic despair would have been
comprehensible to Eleanor, and she would
have sympathized as well as pitied. But
the things she had lost, and the loss of
which had reduced her to what she was,
were so small; at least, they appeared so
to the other. It was not for moral and
spiritual degradation that she mourned
and refused to be comforted, but for material trouble,—vanity crushed, great hopes

of advancement and aggrandizement shat‑
tered; her social position, such as it was,
gone for ever, and humbler women who
had been clever enough to take care
of themselves, exalted above her. When
they showed her her child, who was a
healthy and beautiful boy, though not
robust, she turned away in horror, with
hatred in her eyes—the nearest approach
to an active emotion which she had shown
since her calamity. It was what Michael
had expected to see, and he noted it down
in his mind.

"I wish he was dead, and me too!" she
said, looking coldly at Michael. "I think
you might have put us both out of the
way, Dr. Langstroth, if you had had as
much kind feeling as people talk about."

Michael told Eleanor that the child
must be removed from Ada's vicinity.
Therefore, while the latter remained at
the farm, in Mrs. Nadin's care, Eleanor
charged herself with the baby, and took

it and its nurse into her house. She could
have devised no surer means of healing
the wounds, sweetening the bitterness,
soothing the angriness of her own thoughts.
The utter helplessness of the child, the
terrible circumstances of its birth, its
clouded future, appealed irresistibly to
her nature. She grew to love the little
creature with an intensity which surprised
herself. She hushed it to sleep in her
arms, or interrogated its large mournful
eyes as they stared upwards, with long,
vacant gaze into her absorbed face. And
in this occupation she had time to ponder
over all that had happened, and to try
to shape her course in accordance, not
with the dictates of anger and passion,
however just, but with the laws of mercy
and forgiveness. The helpless figure in
her arms, whose warm and clinging de-
pendence seemed to make everything more
human and more endurable, softened her,
calmed her, so that sometimes she spoke

to Michael of what had happened, and of what might happen, with an insight and a depth of thought and feeling which surprised him, ready as he was to credit her with all manner of goodness and nobleness.

Her great desire, during the period in which the boy was under her care, was to get a marriage performed between Otho and Ada. Thorsgarth was not an entailed property, though it had always been the practice in the Askam family to arrange it and the succession to it as if it had been. If Otho and Ada were married, and he could be forced to do justice to this child, though he could never give him the name he ought to have borne, yet much evil would be removed, and great sorrow and heartburning averted.

Strange to say, the difficulties in the way of this scheme arose, not with Otho, but with Ada. When the latter was well enough to leave the farm, Eleanor brought

her to her own house, since Ada utterly
refused to go home, saying she would kill
herself if they took her there.

Through Gilbert, she and Michael had
word that Otho was subdued, cowed, and
changed; that it had become a sort of
superstitious wish with him to have the
marriage consummated. This gave hope
to Eleanor. But Ada, when questioned,
merely said, with profound melancholy,
and profound indifference, "What does
it matter? If he married me fifty times,
he cannot give me back any of the things
that made me happy. I do not care what
any one thinks or says. Father says he
will remove from here, and let me live
with him. That will do as well as
anything."

So firmly was she planted in this mind,
that after a time they ceased to press it
upon her, trusting to time to work a change.
At the end of March she was still at
the Dower House, seeing only Eleanor,

Michael, and her father, who sometimes
came to visit her. Mr. Dixon was a broken
man now. His wife's anger took a different shape from his; she would have
had him sell his business and retire altogether from a place where they could never
hold up their heads again. But the poor
old man was not thus to be torn away
from his child, or from the place where she
was. Mrs. Dixon indignantly refused to
see the baby; but her husband frequently
stole up to the Dower House of an afternoon or evening, creeping timidly into the
room where his daughter sat, and taking
a place beside her. And here he used to
nurse his little grandchild upon his knee,
trying to disguise from Ada the delight he
could not help taking in its looks and
ways, as, when he had once or twice called
her attention to them, she had looked at
him and at the child, too, in a strange way,
of which Eleanor took more notice than
he did; and, warned by Michael, she was

ever on her guard. But it was not written
that Ada was to fulfil her lot in any way
such as they sometimes dimly dreaded.
Her thoughts strayed within her darkened
mind, and as she saw the spring outside
breaking around her, and beheld also the
looks and gestures by which Michael and
Eleanor sometimes betrayed, amidst all
the gloom, that they loved, and were happy,
Ada might have cried also—

"Oh, dark, dark, dark, amidst the blaze of noon!"

Most likely, the intelligence of a certain
order which her woe seemed to have developed in her, read their fears, and smiled
at them. They thought she planned nothing for the future, any more than she
revived at any sign in the present; but in
this they were mistaken.

CHAPTER XIII.

"LET ME ALONE."

As soon as she had been able to brace
herself up to it, about three weeks after
Ada's return, Eleanor had driven to Balder
Hall to see Magdalen, who was, of course,
acquainted with what had happened. While
Miss Askam could not restrain her sobs
and tears when she came to speak of these
things, Miss Wynter maintained her usual
impassive calm. What she felt about it,
none could have told. She asked many
questions which Eleanor, keenly feeling
her right to be informed in the matter,
answered freely; but she was very quiet
and calm, and made scarce any comments

upon it all, and let Eleanor go away, scarcely replying to the offers of friendship and sympathy on the part of the latter. Eleanor had mentioned Miss Strangforth, to which Magdalen replied very quietly—

"Miss Strangforth is dying. I fear there is no doubt about that, though Michael would scarcely be likely to mention it to you in your other troubles. It is a question of time only, he tells me— and not a very long time."

"And then—you?"

"I—oh, I shall get on somehow. I am not afraid."

"But promise me that if you are not decided, you will come to me till you know something."

"I will see. I appreciate your kindness, but I can promise nothing," said Magdalen; but to the great surprise of Eleanor, she stooped her proud head, and lightly kissed her visitor's cheek.

With this unaccustomed salute still ting-

ling there—now hot, now cold—Eleanor
drove home, with what cheer she might.

A short time after this, just about
Christmas, Miss Strangforth died. Her
place was empty at last, and there was to
be a place made for the heir to step in.
Eleanor wondered what would happen to
Magdalen, and at last received news
through Michael. She was going to remain at Balder Hall. Mr. Strangforth,
the new owner, was a middle-aged man,
with an invalid wife. He was, of course,
distantly related to Magdalen herself.
He had a family of boys and girls, who
wanted much looking after, and he had
asked Miss Wynter to remain, and manage
the household as she had always done. It
seemed a strange post for the haughty
young woman, who had been almost too
proud to set foot outside her aunt's park.
She had accepted Mr. Strangforth's offer,
and said she would call to see Eleanor
as soon as she had time. At present she

was so busy preparing for the newcomers
that she could not leave the house.

"Oh," exclaimed Eleanor, "is he a nice
man, Michael ?   Will he be kind to her ?"

"He is a very sedate, grave kind of man
—almost austere.   But he is a gentleman,
and he will behave becomingly towards
her, I am certain.   He quite appreciates
her devotion to his aunt, and told me he
should always provide for her in a way
suitable to her condition and his family,
whatever that may mean."

Eleanor was very thoughtful about this.
She seemed to see Magdalen—and yet
she could not believe that it would ever
be so—growing into one of those women
whose lives are all behind them ; gradually
becoming old and more stately, more
monumental as the years went by ; so that
at last no one would imagine, to look at
her, that she had been the centre of such
passions as she had caused, or moved in ;
so that no one but herself and a few others,

grown old with her, would know how
hotly her heart had beaten, at the same
time that other old hearts had throbbed,
which with time had grown chill.

And at this time, at the end of March,
a change took place in the circumstances
of all, and the marriage which Eleanor
had grown so anxious for, took place—but
not until a little later, in April.

Gilbert wrote to Michael, and said that
he and Otho were coming to Thorsgarth;
that Otho's affairs were now in such
a state that something must be done about
them. He had, it would seem, run his
course, and it was necessary to see what
could be retrieved in his estate. They
were, of course, coming very quietly, and
would stay as short a time as possible,
bringing the solicitor of the Askam family
with them, as there were certain papers
at Thorsgarth which it was necessary to
overhaul. He wished Eleanor to know
this, as Otho was still in his cowed and

subdued state, and ready to go through the marriage with Ada, if she could be persuaded to it.

Eleanor waited till she had heard that they had actually arrived at Thorsgarth, and then shut herself up with Ada, and combated her objections in such wise, and placed the matter in such a light, that Ada at last exclaimed—

"Very well! Give me peace! Since you say it will do so much good, let us try it."

The words haunted her hearer for some time, but she felt that her purpose was genuine. Some of the reproach would be wiped away, and the future of the child would at any rate be rendered somewhat more hopeful. She at once communicated with Gilbert, and Mr. Johnson, and a special license having been procured, Otho Askam and Ada Dixon were made man and wife, in the drawing-room of the Dower House, one

showery April morning. Eleanor noticed
how, during the service there was a
violent shower of rain, which beat against
the pane, while the sunlight fell on the
trees in the square outside, and how, at
the sound of the falling water, Ada lifted
her face to the window, and looked with
a strange look towards the sky.

Eleanor found her eyes dragged towards
Otho, by a power stronger than her own
will. She was struck with the change
in him. He had grown old-looking : his
shoulders were bowed ; his head drooped.
He glanced from one to the other of
them, with a shifty, cowed expression ; and
his eyes every now and then wandered
towards Ada, who was perhaps the only
person in the room who neither saw nor
looked at him. When it was over, and
Gilbert, who had been at his side through
it all, took his arm to lead him away, he
wiped the sweat from his brow, and looked
all about him, and at Gilbert, and at

Ada, with a white, scared face, and moved uncertainly, as if he could not see.

When every one had gone, except Mr. Dixon, Eleanor went to Ada, stooped over her chair, and said—

"Now, Ada, the worst is over. You may have something to live for yet."

Ada looked at her with one of those prolonged, vacant gazes, which seemed to Eleanor to come from somewhere far on the other side of the tomb, and shaking her head, merely replied—

"Let me alone now. I've done what you wanted. I am satisfied. Next time, I will do what *I* want."

CHAPTER XIV.

HOW ADA SOLVED HER PROBLEM.

IT was a week after the marriage, and during that week much business had been accomplished, and many plans laid. Ever since that day, a change had been perceptible in Ada—a change which, by contrast with her late gloom, might almost have been called brightness. She noticed persons and things, and once or twice voluntarily addressed herself to others.

Gilbert had been in communication with Eleanor, on business affairs, and it was decided that Thorsgarth need not be sold, if Eleanor chose to make an allowance to her brother and to Ada, which she was

very willing to do, so long as Otho agreed
to absent himself from her neighbourhood
and that of Ada, wherever they might be.
He was ready enough to promise this.
His fear and dread seemed to have turned
into an indifference in which considerable
irritability displayed itself. But for the
strong head and hand of Gilbert keeping
him in check, it seemed as if Otho, once
secure of a subsistence, would have taken
his departure from the scene, and left
those behind him to settle his affairs as
they could, or would. This, however, he
was not permitted to do, but was kept
on the spot until everything was arranged,
the agreements drawn up and signed,—a
ceremony which took place at the Dower
House, in the presence of Otho, Eleanor,
Gilbert, Mr. Coningsby of Bradstane, Mr.
Palfreyman of London, and the requisite
witnesses.

By the new arrangement Eleanor would
be practically left with only two or three

hundred a year at her disposal, instead of the ample income of twelve or thirteen hundred a year which she had hitherto enjoyed. In another state of things this might have troubled her, but now it failed to do so in the least. Discussing the circumstance one day with Michael she smilingly said something about his being tied to a pauper, to which Michael replied in a very matter-of-course tone, that as soon as everything was settled, and Otho gone away, and Ada retired to her father's house, he intended Eleanor and himself to be married.

" The sooner you enter upon your life of pauperism, the better," he remarked.

Eleanor made no opposition ; her feeling was one of thankfulness that instead of coming in the style of the orthodox lover, and asking her what she would like to do, he simply told her what was going to be done. Her trust in him was entire and without flaw or reservation, and from this course on his part she perceived that his trust in her was of the same nature as hers in him. She might have echoed the words of the heroine in "Wuthering Heights," who cried, "Do I love Heathcliff? Why, I *am* Heathcliff!" So Eleanor felt with regard to Michael. That which they had passed through together, the fate which after so short an acquaintance, had thrown them, across every obstacle, into the closest intimacy, had developed perfection of sympathy, and a oneness of heart and mind, which sometimes only comes with years of married life, sometimes never comes at all.

On the evening of that day when the final settlements had taken place, Gilbert came to the Dower House, and related how all was decided, and how, the day after to-morrow, they were returning to town, Otho having consented to remain a day longer, as Gilbert had business to settle at the mills. These arrangements,

and Ada's prospective departure, were
discussed openly and purposely in Ada's
presence on this particular evening, and
though she did not speak, she seemed to
listen attentively to what was said. By-
and-by Gilbert went away, saying that
he would see Eleanor once again before
he left Bradstane altogether, as he had
something that he particularly wished to
say to her.

During the forenoon of the following
day Michael called at the Dower House.
Ada presently left him and Eleanor alone,
but in a few minutes returned, dressed, to
the surprise of both, in bonnet and shawl,
as if she intended going out. Both looked
up in astonishment. Ada's face wore an
expression of something like hopefulness.
It was still so different from her former
face, that scarcely any one would have
recognized it who had been unacquainted
with the history of what had happened
during the last year. That is to say, it

was now no longer the face of a girl, but
the set, formed countenance of a woman
who has suffered, and whose sufferings
have hardened, not softened her.   But
to-day it wore a look of expectancy, almost
of animation.

"Dr. Langstroth," said she, " I'm going
to ask a great favour of you."

"Are you, Ada ?   I am glad to hear it."

" It is, that if you've a little time to
spare, you'd walk with me through the
town.   You see, you have that character
that whatever you choose to do, you may
do ; you won't lose any reputation by
being seen with me.   I — I've been
thinking that when you and Miss Askam
are married, and I go back to father and
mother, I cannot bear the long days in
the house there, as I have done here.   It
would drive me mad.   But if I'm left to
myself, I shall never have the courage to
walk out alone.   I thought, if you'd go
out with me this once, just down the town,

then perhaps I might not be afraid to find my way back alone, over the old bridge and up here again, if you do not mind."

This was by far the longest speech Ada had made since she had been under Eleanor's roof, and Michael watched her attentively as she spoke, and noticed that she did not meet his eye.

"Mind!" he echoed, rising; "no, I do not mind, Ada. I am very glad to find you disposed to make this beginning. Let us go. Miss Askam will spare me."

"Surely, Michael!" said Eleanor; but she looked at him anxiously, for her keen sympathy told her that he was not altogether easy about this decision of Ada's. She looked at him earnestly, and her fears were not lulled when she found that he avoided looking at her, though he waved his hand a little, and smiled, saying they should not be long.

"Oh, Michael, take care of *yourself*," she whispered in his ear; to which he nodded, and followed Ada out of the room. Eleanor watched them from the window, and saw that they walked slowly.

Two minutes after they had gone, Gilbert came in.

"You are alone," he said; "I am not sorry, Eleanor, for I want to say something to you."

"Yes, Gilbert," said she, and he was surprised when she took the hand he extended into both her own, and pressing it almost convulsively said, rapidly, and with a kind of passion in her tones— "Another time I will see you alone— whenever you like; and if you have any favour to ask of me, I swear I will grant it; but oh, Gilbert, listen to me, now. Ada has asked Michael to take her for a walk through the town, because she dare not go alone. I know he thinks she is going to try to do something dreadful, because she is not sane, though she seems so; he told me so. Perhaps to kill herself,

or him. Who can answer for the fancies
of a madwoman? I hate her sometimes."

"Well?" he echoed, looking down into
her upturned face, which seemed to blaze
with emotion, and feeling a spasm contract
his own heart.

"Will you not follow them, Gilbert, dear
Gilbert? For my sake, if it is not too
selfish of me to ask it. If you will not
go, I must. I cannot tell why I feel this
agony of fear, but I do, and it masters me.
To please me, Gilbert; and I will do what
I can to please you, afterwards."

She had pressed more closely to him,
her eyes strainingly fixed upon his face,
her whole frame trembling. Her agitation
communicated itself to Gilbert, like some
subtle electric thrill. Over his blue-gray
eyes there was a kind of film, and a tremor
in his voice, as he said.—

"For your sake, my sister . . . but . . .
if anything hinders me from seeing you
again to-day, Eleanor, good-bye."

He stooped his head, and his lips rested for a second, no more, upon her brow. And then she was alone again.

* * * * *

Michael and Ada walked slowly down the sloping square, where they saw scarcely any one. Then, turning a corner, they emerged in the main street of the old town, which also sloped steeply downhill. The sunlight was streaming gaily upon this street; the shops were open, and many people were moving to and fro. In it were situated the house of Ada's father, her former home; the schoolroom in which the concert had taken place, and several other public buildings—all clustering together, in homely vicinity, as they do in towns of this size. As they proceeded down this street they, of course, attracted notice. It was not a usual thing to see Michael walking in a leisurely manner down the town at that hour of the day. And it was more than a year since his companion had been seen in the places where her figure had once been familiar. People looked at them—came to their doors in curiosity, and gazed at and after them, and Michael knew that his companion was trembling from head to foot. Her face was deadly pale ; her eyes were fixed upon the ground. But she neither hurried, nor faltered in her step, walking straight onwards, down the hill, and towards the mills. When they were nearly there, and the number of people who were about had sensibly diminished, he spoke to her, for the first time, quietly and tranquilly—

" Now, Ada, shall we return ? I think you have walked far enough."

" Not that way," she replied, in a fluttering voice. " I can't face it again. We'll cross the footbridge, and go round the other side, where it's quieter."

He humoured her, and they went through the dark passage, and emerged on the bridge.

"Now," said she, "won't you turn back, sir? I don't want to keep you, and I can go well enough by myself this way. It is very quiet."

"Yes, very quiet," replied he composedly. "I will walk round with you. My time is quite at your disposal."

She hesitated for a moment, and he saw that she looked at him in a stealthy, side-long manner, of which he took no notice, openly. Happening to turn his head, he saw Gilbert just behind them. He wondered how he had got there, but felt a sense of relief in knowing that he was present, and obeying a sign of his brother's hand, took no notice of him.

Midway over the bridge, Ada walked more slowly, raised her head, and began to look about her.

"Why," she observed, "the river is in spate; that's the rains up by Cauldron, I suppose?"

"Yes," said Michael; and, indeed, there

was a wild, if a joyous prospect around
them. April green on the woods and
grass, and April sunshine in the sky, and
the river, which was as she said, in spate,
tearing along, many feet higher than usual,
with brown, turbid waters, looking resist-
less in their swiftness and their strength.

" Well," she next observed, in a muffled
voice, " it's far worse than I thought, and
not better, as Miss Askam said it would
be. It makes me sure that I'm right."

" Right in what, Ada ? "

" In what I thought about facing the
people again."

" It is the first step that costs. In time
you will mind it less. It is well that you
tried it."

" Perhaps it is. It is well to make sure
of things," said Ada, in a stronger voice.
" But I'll never do it again. I'll never be
stared at and whispered about in that
way, any more. They would like to
throw stones at me, if they dared. If I'd

been alone, I dare say they would have done."

"You wrong them——"

"What does it matter?" she said coldly, as she stooped to pick a tuft of small flowers from the grassy bank of the river. Then she paused a moment, picking them to pieces, and seemed absorbed in reflection upon what she had felt in passing through the town. Suddenly she looked up at Michael, and said—

"There's one thing I should like to say, Dr. Langstroth. *You* are a man, whatever the rest may be; and I always knew you were; and it was because I always felt you were so high above me that I used to say such ill-natured things of you to Roger. I knew that you saw through me, if he didn't; but you never betrayed me. However, it will be all the same to you. I can't hurt you or help you, one way or another—so good-bye."

With that she slipped past him, with a

darting movement which eluded his grasp,
ran down the bank of the river, stood for
one moment poised for the spring she took,
and the next instant he saw her swept like
a reed, many yards away, down the giant
current of the stream.

" Fool that I was !" he muttered, turning
instinctively to rush down the stream, and
if possible, go beyond her, before he
plunged in, so that he could meet and
intercept her.   But Gilbert meι him at the
corner of the bridge.   There was a curious
look in his eyes and his hand held back
Michael by the arm, with a grip in which
the latter felt powerless.

" Your way is over the bridge," he said.
" Go and meet us.   Eleanor sent *me*."

It had scarce taken two seconds to say
and do ; and Gilbert had plunged into the
stream also.   The current instantly washed
both figures across to the other bank.
Michael rushed across the bridge, and
down the other side, pale ; a surging in

his ears ; his heart thumping, so that his laboured breath could scarce come. Dimly he saw that other forms met him at the bridge end, and followed him ; vaguely he heard a hum of voices behind him. He pursued his way, panting, blind with fear. Ever and anon the noise of the river seemed to swell into a roar like thunder, which quenched all other sounds. Here and there a growth of bushes and willows hid the waters from him ; but at last, as he stumbled onwards, and rounded one of the curves in that much curved stream, his straining eyes caught sight of something— human forms, surely—arrested by a rock which projected midway into the current.

" He has got to shore, and brought her with him," a thought seemed to say. " He is too exhausted to drag himself out. I shall soon be with him now."

But, without knowing it, he began to sob and sob and sob as he approached ; and when he drew near, instead of going swiftly to the place, he strayed around and about it, and could not, dared not go close.

It seemed long, very long before he could understand. Other persons, who had seen what had happened, or part of it, and who had seen Michael rush after the other two, had come up, and they told him again and again. A score of times he heard the words repeated: " Dead ; both dead. No one could swim in such a flood!" And yet he did not grasp it. But at last, after what seemed a long time, it did come home to him, and he understood that Ada had avenged herself.

CHAPTER XV.

MAGDALEN. IN VALEDICTION.

IT was July of the same year, and the time drew towards evening. The bright, westering sun was shining into the library at the Red Gables. In one of the deep window-seats, Eleanor and Michael sat side by side, and hand in hand. It seemed as if he had just returned from some journey, for there were signs about the room of a traveller's recent arrival; and she, it would appear, had not even yet done bidding him welcome, her eyes dwelling still, with undiminished light of affection upon a face beloved. They had been man and wife for three weeks, and after a short ten days of honeymoon, he had brought her home, and left her there, while he went to London, to attend to the innumerable affairs connected with his brother's business, will, and death. Ten minutes ago he had come in, and she was asking him for his news, which he seemed almost unwilling to enter upon.

" There are letters for me, I perceive," he said at last. " That is from Roger. When did it come ? "

" This morning only."

" Let me have it."

" No. I have read it. It will keep, because it contains good news. I want to know first all you have not told me. The good news for the last."

" I have told you almost everything, my child. It has been a sad business ; sad from beginning to end. I have settled it all up—all poor Gilbert's affairs. He was different from me ; no doubt of that. I learnt a lesson or two."

" In what way ? "

"Why, Eleanor, it is simply the old story, that a man often seems much worse than he is. I never for a moment realized that *I* could have been in fault. I always saw his sin so large ; it blotted out everything else. We will talk it all over another time. There was no difficulty in settling his affairs ; disorder was abhorrent to his very soul. When I think of that, and of his painstaking, methodical, perfect system of doing things, and then remember my own scatterbrained practices, and remember how young he was, too, I feel as if now, by the light of all these other troubles and experiences, I can understand the temptation that beset him then, to keep things safe—the returning prosperity which he had built up with so much trouble—to keep me from squandering it, as he felt sure I should. Yes ; I can see it. By George ! What an opinion I must have had in those days of my own per-

fection and freedom from flaw of any
kind. It is incredible."

" But, Michael, it was wrong of him."

" Yes, it was wrong of him, and as
wrong of me. Roger knew that. Roger
was very unhappy because of what I did.
We were both about as wrong as we could
be, I suppose."

Eleanor was silent. She would not
gainsay him, but she did not agree ; and
it was hardly to be expected that she
should at that stage of the proceedings.

" His will, Eleanor, will surprise you.
It was made since that Christmas when
you and he were together at Thorsgarth ;
when Magdalen and Otho became engaged. And he has left his money rather
curiously,—half to Magdalen, in case she
marries Otho, to be settled upon her and
her children if she should have any, as
strictly as it can possibly be done ; and
half to you, in case you marry—whom, do
you suppose ? "

"Not himself?" she asked, pale and breathless.

Michael laughed.

"No, madam, but your present husband."

"Michael! And what if——"

"If neither of those marriages really took place, it all came to me, except an annuity to Magdalen of five hundred a year."

"To Magdalen!"

"Yes. I, too, was surprised at first. And then I seemed to comprehend that too. It was for the sake of old times, when we were young together. He and Magdalen in a cool, curious sort of way, always understood one another; and when he was over here, he several times spoke to me about her, and seemed distressed at the idea of the great change and reverse that had come over her. 'She is not a high-minded woman,' he said to me once, 'but she has had every hope crushed, and has lived in a kind of tomb with that old

woman all the best of her life.' So that
was the way he took, I suppose, of ex-
pressing his sympathy."

"It is wonderful," said Eleanor in a
low voice, feeling humbled, puzzled, and
ashamed. This view of Magdalen's life
had never intruded itself into her mind.
And it was as if she heard a voice echoing
in the air about her, "Judge not!"

"Yes, it is wonderful, and very hum-
bling to me. And to you also, he left this
ring."

He took a case from his breast-pocket,
and gave it to her. It contained a ring
set with a large pearl of unusual size and
beauty, surrounded by brilliants, in a fine
and delicate small pattern.

"He wished you to wear it always,"
said Michael in a low voice. "This was
in a private letter to me, half finished,
which he must have left amongst his other
papers when he came down here with
Otho, just before that wedding. He said

it was more like his idea of you than anything he had ever seen."

Eleanor was weeping silently as Michael
placed this ring upon her hand.

"Why did he think of me in that way?"
she whispered between her tears. "It
was so wrong, so unlike the truth. It
makes me afraid. I shall always feel that
I am a renegade when I look at it."

"It made him a great deal happier, at
any rate," said Michael gently. "And·
now, Eleanor, something else. I saw
Otho while I was in town."

"Yes?" she said in a slow, reluctant
whisper.

"Well, he is indeed a broken man. His
sins have come home to him, and Ada
avenged herself fearfully; but how, do
you suppose?"

She shook her head.

"Not by her own death; he hardly
alluded to it. That whole connection with
Ada was the merest freak. It is, as it

were, by chance alone—that awful chance which we call Destiny—that that caprice has had such effects for us all. It is, through Gilbert's death, and his alone. It sounds odd to say such a thing of the regard of one man for another, but one might almost say that his affection for Gilbert has been the one love of his life——"

"I know what you mean; and it is so, in a way. Gilbert had more of his heart and soul than any one else—even Magdalen."

"Yes, even Magdalen; for he trifled and played with her, and in fact, mastered her even in coming round to her wishes; but Gilbert, never. It was like the love of a dog for its master. It has knocked him down completely; he has no spirit left. He said there was nothing to live for when a fellow's friend was gone, and he gave some dark hint as to being Gilbert's murderer. I did not stay long with him. I don't know what will become of him. It was absolutely necessary that I should see him on business; so I saw him, and had done with him."

" Did he say nothing about Ada's little child, and its death ? "

" Not a word; and I did not, either. It seemed to me a desecration to mention such things to him."

" Yes. Let us not speak of him. We cannot do anything for him. He would not let us; and for years to come I do not think I could bear to look upon his face. That is all I want to know. Let us read Roger's letter now. He has got a great post, and is going to take a long holiday with us in the autumn; and then he is going to South America to manage a business there for the people he is now with."

"Ah! His career, that I have prophesied for him, is beginning then," said Michael, as he read Roger's letter with her, seated

beside her, each of them holding a leaf.
And as they sat thus, with that softened
look upon their faces which comes with
thoughts of a much-loved absent one, the
door opened, and the servant announced
Miss Wynter.

They both looked up in surprise as she
entered.   She walked up to the table and
stood looking at them with a keen, searching gaze, and her lips quivered a little as
she saw the attitude of entire trust, and
the look of peace and of rest upon both
faces.   Magdalen, like the others, was in
black ; she was still clad in the deep
mourning she had been wearing for Miss
Strangforth ; perhaps in her soul she was
not sorry that circumstances allowed her
to wear a garb so well according with her
own feelings.   But it struck Eleanor that
she was equipped for a longer journey
than that from Balder Hall to the Red
Gables.   Her face was very pale, but there
was no abatement—there never had been

any abatement—in the pride of its expression. Whatever Magdalen's fate, she would always carry it, to all outward seeming, with the stateliness of a queen who wears her crown.

" You were so absorbed, you scarcely heard my name," she said in her clear, rather sarcastic tones, and with a slight cool smile. " I am glad to find you in. I heard that Michael was coming home to-day, and I did not wish to go away without saying good-bye."

" You are going away ? " said Eleanor. " Are you going for long ? "

" Most likely I shall never see you again," Magdalen pursued. " It is not probable that our paths will ever cross. Indeed, I shall make it my object to prevent them from doing so."

" Magdalen——"

But Michael, a little better acquainted with human nature, and especially with Magdalen's nature, than was his wife, had already guessed, and his eyes were fixed upon Miss Wynter's face, scrutinizingly, but with little surprise.

"I am going to London," said Magdalen. "I intend travelling there by the south mail this evening. I have sent my things on, and called to see you on my way to the station."

"To London—— " began Eleanor.

Magdalen's eyebrows contracted. She gave a short, impatient laugh.

"How long you are in comprehending! I see Michael understood at once. Ah, Michael, if you had understood me as well seven years ago! . . . Well, Eleanor, I am going to Otho."

"To Otho!"

"Yes, to Otho. When I promised to marry him, I swore that when the time came, I would follow him faithfully, no matter how or where. He said we should both know when it had come. It has come now. Since he saw you in town, Michael,

I have heard from him. He has taken some rooms for me, and I shall go and stay there ; and as soon as I have been there long enough, we shall be married."

Eleanor was silent at first. Then she began, tremulously—

" Have you thought seriously about it ? After what has happened, he can have no claim upon you; and you surely do not dare to go to him."

" Dare—I dare, most certainly, go to him, and stay with him. I am not afraid of him. I never was. If some other people had been as little afraid of him as I was, perhaps he might not have made such a hideous bungle as he has done, of his life. But if I were afraid of him, I should go to him all the more, after what I swore to him, lest he should do me some hurt if I disobeyed him."

" But, Magdalen—— "

" But, Eleanor !" said the other, in a deep, stern voice. " Let me explain my-

self, and then, if you fail to understand, it
will not be my fault. I am going to him
now, first because of my promise, which
meant, that when there should be nothing
to prevent me from marrying him, I would
be his wife. And what is there to prevent
me now ?"

" There is himself!" cried Eleanor pas-
sionately. " Michael, tell her—explain to
her that she must not tie——"

" Wait! She has not finished yet," said
Michael.

" No, I have not," Magdalen assented.
" First, because of my promise to him.
You think that because himself, as you call
it, frightened and repelled you, it must, of
course, be the same with every one else.
Well, while I am about it, I will tell you
the whole truth. He has not a friend in
the world, I suppose, now that Gilbert is
gone, except me. I am in the same case.
While my poor old aunt still lived, there
was always some one who believed in me,

and thought I was an angel. There is no one now. Himself—such as he is—loves me, with such love as he has to give; clings to me, and wants me. And I—such as I am—infinitely beneath you, I confess " (with a mocking smile and bow), " love him, with what heart has not been crushed out of me. Yes, and such as he is," she added, raising herself before them, and looking at them with a kind of defiance on her scornful face—" such as he is, I think it worth while to go to him, and try to save him from destruction. Perhaps I shall not succeed. That doesn't matter. I want something to do, and there it is, ready to my hand. . . . And also, I shall then have kept a promise to one man, at any rate."

Eleanor stared at her, half-fascinated, half-repelled.

" One word to you, Michael," added Magdalen. " You look happy now, as I have never seen you look before; and I firmly believe you will be happy. You must have forgiven me long ago for not having married you; and now I should think you join thankfulness to forgiveness. But I wish to tell you that I know I behaved vilely to you—not in breaking off our engagement, but in ever making it; and you treated me better than most men would treat a woman who has cheated them, and then made a mess of her affairs. I wronged you, and I deserve what I have got for it. That is more than I would own to any one else in the world. It will serve as my wedding-present to you, Eleanor; there is no testimony to goodness so strong as that which is offered by what is—not goodness. And now," she added, looking at the clock, " it is time for me to go. I should like to shake hands with you both, and wish you good-bye."

In her attitude, as she turned towards them, there was something imposing. There was neither softness, nor benignity, nor true nobility—the nobility of soul, that is—in any of her looks or gestures; but there was a certain still, unbending pride, and a dauntless, unquailing gaze into the iron eyes of misfortune which thrilled them both. Eleanor took her hand between both her own, and looked long, earnestly, speechlessly into her face, saying at last—

"Magdalen, why do you delight to make yourself out a worse woman than you are? Is it nothing that you have done, to live with Miss Strangforth as you did, and treat her so that she thought you an angel? nothing in what you are going to do? For it is a martyrdom to which you doom yourself, say what you please."

"No, it isn't," said Magdalen, with a harsh laugh, looking with a curious expression into Eleanor's eyes. "That's why I am not a good woman, Eleanor. It is no martyrdom at all. I am glad, I am *glad* I am going—going to get away from this hateful place, and be married to Otho.

And if I had got married to Michael, long
before he ever saw you, child, I should
have been a miserable woman, and should
most likely have done something out-
rageous, sooner or later. That's where
the badness comes in. Good - bye,
Michael."

"Let me come to· the train and see you
off," he said.

"No, certainly not. You mean to be
kind, I know ; but I am going alone. If
I fancied you were looking after me, I
might look back, and not be so delighted
with my future as I ought."

"Then, Magdalen, give it up, and stay
with——" began Eleanor eagerly, as she
stepped forward with outstretched hands.
But the other had gone swiftly out of the
room, without looking back, and had closed
the door after her.

Eleanor turned to her husband, who was
looking at her. They confronted each
other for a moment or two, till she asked—

"Is she a heroine, or is she—Michael, what is she?"

"She is Magdalen Wynter," he answered. "I don't know what she is; but there is certainly some heroine in her."

"To marry Otho!" murmured Eleanor.

"I think she is just doing what she said herself, going to work with the thing nearest her hand—anything to get away from here. And it takes the shape of heroism, because, you know, she will never let him sink; at least, she will be always struggling to keep him straight—what they call straight," said Michael, and his voice was not quite steady. "Magdalen always laughed at heroism," he added.

"God help her!" said Eleanor in a low voice.

*   *   *   *   *

The factories by the river have now been long disused. Most likely Michael will some time follow the once despised advice of honest Sir Thomas Winthrop, and pull them down. As they stand now, silent and quiet, footsteps echo through the passage which leads to the bridge, and Tees goes murmuring past the spot, telling, as it seems to our imperfect ears, the same story exactly that it has been telling for so many hundred years. Whether what we call inanimate nature stands blindly by, without taking any impress from the scenes which humanity acts in the arena she prepares for them, is one of the mysteries which we cannot solve. To us, the trees appear the same each year, and the voice of the river changes only with the seasons, and with periods of drought or flood. A shriek, once uttered, is lost, and death is the end of all things.

Long letters come from Roger to the friends at the Red Gables, telling of prosperity and advancement, speaking of love unchanged to them and theirs, but never hinting at any thoughts of returning to his native land.

Ada's child, which pined and died not long after she did, is buried in her grave; and Gilbert also sleeps in Bradstane churchyard.

As for the two who were left alone of all this company who had been young at the same time, the years brought changes in their life, and ofttimes in their habitations. But since this chronicle professes only to deal with that part of their lives which was played out in the Borderland where they dwelt, it is not necessary to follow those changes, but only to say that they still speak of Bradstane and the Red Gables as "home." For humane and kindly hearts always find loves and interests; hopes and occupations spring thickly around them, on every side and in every soil; and so it was with these two. Human interests and hopes, keen and deep, bind them to the old spot. There are those there, both old and young, whom they love, and who love them, and from whose vicinity they would not, if they could, tear themselves altogether.   These things, and a certain righteousness of thought and deed in their own lives, have mercifully dimmed and blurred the memories of one or two tragic years, and have restored most of its loveliness and much of its freshness to life ; have done for their bitterer remembrances exactly what the abundant ivy and the gracious growth of flowers and ferns have done for the naked grimness of the castle ruins which stand on the cliff above the river.

THE END.

PRINTED BY WILLIAM CLOWES AND SONS, LIMITED,
LONDON AND BECCLES.

www.ingramcontent.com/pod-product-compliance
Lightning Source LLC
Chambersburg PA
CBHW020856020726
47497CB00005B/1439